Grab a FR

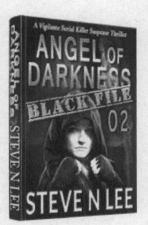

You get *Black File 02* free with this book (see Table of Contents for details).

Angel of Darkness

Angel of Darkness Book 02

Steve N. Lee

Copyright

Published by Blue Zoo, Yorkshire, England.

Angel of Darkness

Chapter 01

THE RIFLE SCOPE prowled across the park with the dead, emotionless gaze of a great white gliding through the murky depths. From a ledge on the roof of the 150-foot-tall granite tomb, the scope scanned the tree-lined pathways extending from the memorial. The crosshairs skimmed over cold, gray paving stones, stark leafless shrubbery, unlit street lights modeled after nineteenth-century gas lamps, and then...

A young, frizzy-haired woman in a baggy red sweater and black leggings read on a wooden bench in the sharp spring sunshine. Her legs were crossed, the top one moving rhythmically as if tapping to music, yet the area was silent but for the occasional rumble of traffic.

She had no earphones so what was she doing?

Like the caress of a lover's hand, the scope ran along her thigh, over the curve of her knee, and down her slender shin. Finally, it fell upon a baby carriage gently rocking back and forth under the motion of the woman's foot.

He could see the baby clearly – all chubby-faced smiles and sparkling eyes. Lying on its back, it reached upward, fingers grasping and twisting and pointing, as if it was talking in a sign language only it could understand.

Why would any reasonable person bring a child into this godforsaken world?

He stared at the baby. At its cheery face. At its futile gestures. At his scope's crosshairs resting on its forehead.

It would be kinder to end it here. Right now. Why subject the poor thing to seventy-odd years of never-ending struggle, suffering, and disappointment?

He lightly squeezed the trigger. Felt the rifle tense to strike, like a coiled cobra baring its fangs. All he had to do was ease the trigger back one tiny fraction of an inch more, and the child would never have to know the agony of being abandoned by a lover, watching its dreams burn, or burying a loved one.

But his finger relaxed. No, he wasn't taking the baby. Let the mother live with her child's anguish year after year after year. Let her drown in the knowledge that she had brought such sorrow into the world.

The scope prowled on.

A fat man half-walked, half-dragged a brown dachshund along the path to the park that flowed from the memorial down the gentle hillside to the Hudson River. The dog scurried to keep up, but when its stumpy legs failed it, the guy tugged on the leash and hauled it closer.

People. God, how he hated people. The world would be so much better without them.

The crosshairs moved over the man, then the dog, then back to the man.

But which would be kinder? To force the dog to find a new home? Or the man to find a new victim upon whom to express his dissatisfaction with life?

As the scope followed man and beast down the path, it skimmed over something. It stopped and backed up.

A teenager with jeans halfway down his ass spray-painted his tag onto a wall. Even though he was here doing something so mind-numbingly inconsequential, he obviously believed he was special, yet the odds were that he'd never done anything to even hint at that, let alone confirm it. He probably figured people needed to know his name. That he mattered. That he was important. Figured he was the kind of guy who deserved to be recognized and would one day have fame thrust upon him.

The sniper delicately applied pressure to the trigger once more.

He could make the kid so unbelievably famous. In just a matter of hours, everyone in Manhattan would know his name. Hell, the story could even go national. Yep, the kid would be as big as a rock star. Leastways for a day or two.

So, which would this loser prefer? A life of endless mundanity and total anonymity? Or one fleeting moment when his name was on everyone's lips?

Then he heard it.

He gasped. A rush of excited anticipation welled up inside him and exploded, flooding his body with the closest thing to joy he could remember.

Forsaking the graffiti artist, he swung the telescoping lens around so quickly that the image was just a muddy blur. He stopped and studied the new view only to find that he'd become lost among the rooftops of Harlem. In his haste, he'd overshot the target.

He drew a deep, steadying breath.

Calmness. Stillness. Patience. Those were the secrets to a successful kill shot.

As his excitement waned, he let the scope pan slowly back in the direction of the park.

And all the while, church bells pealed announcing the happy union of two people who were so desperately in love they needed a piece of paper to prove it.

Finally, the crosshairs found Riverside Church's gigantic stone tower, so gigantic it was more like a mini-skyscraper than a humble bell tower. The scope crawled down, down, down the stone wall, interrupted intermittently by the bare branches of the trees lining one of the pathways in between him and it.

Eventually, it came to the crowd of impeccably dressed people gathered on the sidewalk. While talking among themselves, few could tear their gaze away from the church entrance, where stone steps led up to heavy wooden doors decorated with black wrought iron curls and swirls.

Moments later, a chisel-jawed hunk in a dark suit and a black woman with a fashion-magazine-cover figure strolled out hand in hand. The crowd cheered and hurled handfuls of rice.

The two lovers stood on the entrance's top step obviously adoring being showered with such attention. Cameras clicked. Flashes flashed. Rice rained.

The scope crawled over the bridegroom. A typical white, entitled asshole. Born into money. Everything handed to him on a plate. The only tangible contribution he'd ever make to the world would be to bring more entitled mouths into it. Just what the world needed.

The crosshairs moved sideways.

10

And there she was - the ever-loving, ever-fawning, two-faced, gold-digging whore. How many men had she had to bang before she finally landed today's soulmate? Twenty? Fifty? A hundred?

In turn, the scope magnified each of their faces. Each of their sickeningly happy, grinning faces.

Hatred quickened his breath and his heart hammered. His muscles tensed so much that he involuntarily gripped the rifle harder. Too hard.

The weapon wobbled as his contempt shook his sharpshooting expertise. So much so that the target disappeared from his scope, and all he saw was part of the tower once more.

He cursed under his breath and dragged a hand up over his brow and back over his short-cropped graying hair. At this distance, gravity would force a projectile to travel in an arc, so to make the perfect kill shot, allowances had to be made for that when aiming. As if that didn't make the shot complicated enough, temperature, altitude, and humidity had to be considered, too. But those weren't the biggest threats. No, that was down to the wind - over a long distance, the tiniest of gusts could alter a bullet's trajectory and literally blow it off course. Being just a hair's breadth off with his calculations could mean being inches off target at the point of impact. He'd only get one clean shot at this, so he couldn't afford to miss. That meant he had to be statue-still.

He closed his eyes. Breathing slowly and deeply, he forced his hatred and anger down. Forced his body to calm. Blanked everything except himself, his weapon, and his target. Gradually, his hands steadied and the scene through the scope was once more still.

Again, the grinning faces taunted him.

So, should he try to take both of them? Or settle for just one?

That was a tough call.

Luckily, he had time to enjoy the spectacle and to make his decision. Or did he? What if they planned on disappearing into the park to have photos taken, or being whisked away to a party by the black limousine waiting at the curb?

No, there was nothing to be gained from waiting.

He took aim, placing the crosshairs at the very top of the target's forehead to allow for drop, so gravity would work in his favor and not against him.

Gently squeezing the trigger just a fraction, he savored the moment as the weapon ached to be unleashed.

He smirked. Almost done.

Chapter 02

ALONE IN MARLOWE'S Grounds, Tess Williams shook her head, sitting at a round table with a white vase in the center holding a plastic pink orchid.

What was wrong with the world? Well, not the world. The world was doing just fine. No, it was people. What the hell was wrong with people?

Cradling her coffee, she closed her blue eyes and drew a deep, relaxing breath in through her nose. She held it, and then let it out slowly through her mouth. She opened her eyes again. The world was just as she'd left it. Sadly.

The aroma of fresh Javan coffee wafted up from her cup. She stared at the wisps of steam for a moment, then looked back over the heads of the customers at the coffee shop's counter and to the wall-mounted television which featured breaking news from Riverside Church, Morningside Heights. The couple couldn't have picked a more beautiful spring morning for a wedding. Nor a more beautiful church. Couldn't fault them there. They must have figured it would be a perfect day.

The woman reporter tried to look concerned, but all Chanel and attitude, was clearly ecstatic at having landed such a high-profile story. She gestured over the police cordon to the church, where a forensics team scoured the steps and detectives spoke with traumatized wedding guests.

She said, "As you can see, Peter, the police have sealed off the area and are investigating what is yet another truly heinous shooting. The third in just seven days."

In the studio, so well-groomed he looked like a waxwork model, the news anchor, Peter, said, "And I believe Channel 7 has obtained some exclusive footage, isn't that right?"

"Yes, Peter. It reveals the full horror of what happened here today."

Peter looked directly into camera. "Sensitive viewers might wish to look away for a moment as this footage contains some disturbing images."

A shaky handheld video appeared with black bars down either side because the cell phone owner hadn't turned the device sideways to film in landscape mode.

While church bells pealed, a guy in a gray Armani suit and a skinny black woman in a white gown that must have cost as much as a small car stood before the aged wooden doors of Riverside Church.

A crowd of well-wishers cheered and showered them with rice.

The male phone owner shouted, "Give her a kiss."

The groom kissed his new wife and then grinned at the crowd as people clapped.

A rifle shot blasted.

The bride crashed backwards into the church doors. Flesh bursting from where her right eye had been. Blood spattering her wedding gown. So bright, so shockingly red against such virginal white.

For a micro-second, the world froze. Then, after the initial moment of the remarkable stillness that shock always brings, panic erupted.

For a few seconds, the picture was a blur of running, the sound a cacophony of screaming.

The phone owner scurried over to the cover of a limousine parked outside the church. Unbelievably, he continued filming and panned his phone across the chaos.

A woman in a long lemon dress dragged her screaming daughter away, but her dress knotted around her legs. She crashed to the sidewalk. Scrambling up, she lifted the girl with one hand, her dress with the other, and then ran for the sanctuary of the church.

Clutching two wailing children to his chest, a young guy sprinted into the road, a woman trailing alongside. A black car blared its horn and swerved. The family didn't even look, but just shot for the cover of the trees of Riverside Park.

All around, guests grappled with each other to flee the carnage.

The camera owner's voice shook as he spoke. "Oh, God. I–I don't know what's happening... It's like... I don't know... someone's shooting and... Oh, God..." He gasped. "Oh, no... Oh, God, no... Angelique."

On the church steps, the groom sat on the unforgiving stone beside his wife. He pulled her lifeless, blood-drenched body to him.

In the background, globs of blood, chunks of brain, and shards of skull slid down the dark church doors like some grotesque artwork by one of the inmates in an institution for the criminally insane.

An older bald man knelt beside him. He looked at all those running for shelter, running to distance themselves from the happy couple whose perfect day they'd been so eager to share.

The man shouted, "Get an ambulance! For God's sake, get an ambulance."

The groom cradled Angelique and sobbed. Tears ran down his cheeks as blood ran into the gutter.

The news anchor reappeared. "That truly is shocking, Janice. And again, ladies and gentlemen, that's a Channel 7 exclusive. As you know, we always strive to be the first to bring you the news that matters. So, Janice, what's the official response to the incident? Do the police suspect it's the work of the Pool Cleaner?"

"Well, Peter, while it's way too early to speculate, it does fit the profile, the incident involving a Caucasian male and an African American female, so initial indications do indeed point to another Pool Cleaner killing, yes. Though there hasn't yet been official confirmation of that, I'm sure it won't be long in coming."

Tess hung her head. It just never stopped. So she could never stop.

She took a last gulp of her coffee, then shutdown her tablet and stuffed it into her black backpack. Her article on gang violence in Little Russia would have to wait. Another story had grabbed the headlines. A story she'd hoped she'd only ever see reported and never have to become a part of. But like that was ever going to have happened.

She strode toward the door. While most people shuffled or loped or lumbered or slouched, Tess flowed, her gait effortless, gliding, like an exquisite Swiss

16

timepiece, each part precision engineered to interact perfectly with the next.

With slabs of gray cloud gnawing away the blue sky, the sharp spring air bit like a starving dog at the boy teasing it. Tess zipped up her black leather jacket as she exited the coffee shop and emerged onto Broadway.

When the average person thought of Broadway, they pictured the razzmatazz of theater shows, seeing famous actors in the flesh, and the excitement of Times Square. Few people realized that the vast proportion of this world-famous landmark was nothing but an ordinary city street, like countless other city streets across the US. Burger joints, delis, banks, cafés, grocery stores... Broadway ran the length of Manhattan and then continued on for miles. To most New Yorkers, Broadway was merely another street. Nothing exotic. Merely functional.

Amid the honking and growling traffic, a yellow cab pulled up to the curb in front of Tess. A fat guy in a gray overcoat struggled out and then waddled down the sidewalk. Within seconds, he became just another nondescript face in the crowd that people passed without even noticing. In a city with a population of eight million, it was easy to disappear, to be but a blur in the shadows of the most vibrant place on Earth.

Tess strode on, scanning the street ahead and registering the situation on autopilot. The usual assortment of pedestrians cluttered the sidewalk, none appearing to deserve more than a cursory glance. A traffic camera clung to a metal pole at the end of the block, surveilling the junction, but if she hugged the building to her left as she approached, she'd be out of its line of sight. Heading north, the tail end of a police cruiser disappeared into the traffic, its distance and direction making it of little consequence. No uniforms patrolled either sidewalk.

Minimal threat.

Not that anyone was looking for her. Especially not the police. Well... they were, they just didn't know it. Because of the expertise with which Tess masked her activities, New York's finest were looking for multiple suspects in connection to a mounting number of unsolved homicide cases. They did not appreciate that all those crimes were the sole responsibility of just one person – her. On the contrary, thanks to the public persona she'd established, more than a few law enforcement officers would swear under oath that she was a model citizen. That persona took a considerable amount of work to maintain, but was worth the effort.

She checked the angle of the traffic camera to ensure it hadn't been altered since the last time she'd passed this way. It hadn't.

No, no one was looking for her. However, in her line of work, she found it best to keep her movements as under-the-radar as possible.

She slunk closer to the wall, to ensure she was outside the range of the camera when she neared it.

Then she saw it.

She sighed. The Pool Cleaner crime scene was active right now. It was imperative she get there as soon as possible, not least to try to catch the detective she'd seen interviewing people in the background on the news broadcast. But...

Not yet within range of the camera, Tess meandered back toward the curb to get the angle she needed. As she passed a newsstand on her right, she looked left. The reflection in the first-floor wall of glass of the Michenner Building revealed a newsstand plastered with newspapers and magazines, a bearded man peering out from inside, and...

Under her breath, she said, "Goddamnit."

She didn't need this now, but could she really sail on by if something was going down?

Chapter 03

TESS STOPPED TEN yards past the newsstand, so as not to raise suspicion, then slipped her phone out of its pouch. The pouch's RF shielding prevented her from being tracked, no matter who was searching for her and what resources they had at their disposal. She pretended to take a call. "Hello."

She dawdled a few more steps, then slowly turned and dawdled back, her gaze casually drifting over the area.

Into her phone, Tess said, "Uh-huh." While talking, she studied the scene, hoping her instincts were wrong. "Sorry, Tuesday doesn't work for me."

Beside the newsstand, someone was acting way too innocent to be innocent.

A tall black guy lurked next to the stand, just out of view of the bearded man behind the counter. Wearing a red puffer jacket, he was so scrawny, he looked like the only thing making him three dimensional was his coat's tire-like ribs. Head down, staring at his phone, he sipped from a mega-sized paper coffee cup emblazoned with the words 'Coffee Shack.' To passersby, he must have looked like just an average guy using his phone. But something didn't feel right.

From the corner of her eye, Tess studied the scrawny guy as he ambled back and forth while checking his messages and sipping his coffee. What the devil was it that was off?

Then it hit her – he was drinking coffee as much as she was taking a phone call.

Again, he lifted the cup to his mouth, touched the rim to his lips, but then lowered it without drinking a single drop. All the while, his eyes flicked from side to side, scanning the sidewalk and the glass building far more than his phone.

Tess had witnessed the spill scam numerous times – a street hustler maneuvered into such a position that an innocent person couldn't help but spill their drink over them, at which point they could demand money to cover cleaning costs.

Tess looked at the guy's cup again. There was no plastic lid on the cup and yet no steam rose from the coffee – this guy had been waiting far too long for it to be that rudimentary scam. No, this was something bigger. Something riskier. Something all together more lucrative.

Tess glanced at her watch. She had to get to Riverside Church as soon as possible. However, she needed a clear head if she was going to tackle the Pool Cleaner, and knowing she'd walked away from this con, without even trying to stop someone from getting burned, would gnaw at her, sapping her concentration. So what choice did she have?

She set a countdown timer on her watch so there would be no question of at what point she had to leave – ten minutes, then she was gone.

The countdown didn't even reach five.

A portly black man shuffled out through the electronic doors of the Michenner Building. Cocooned in a gray suit that must have cost a grand if it cost a buck, he chuckled as he talked on his phone. He headed back down the street the way Tess had come, engrossed in his call.

The scrawny guy shot from beside the newsstand. It looked like the portly man was the mark he'd been waiting for.

As Scrawny Guy neared the mark, he called out, "Hey, buddy."

It was obviously well-practiced because it was loud enough that someone in the mark's position should register it, but quiet enough that they'd think it wasn't directed at them.

The mark didn't turn but continued down the street.

Scrawny Guy closed in. Once almost on top of the mark, he called again, much louder, while holding up what looked like a hundred-dollar bill. "Buddy, you dropped this."

As the mark turned around, Scrawny Guy jerked forward so the pair of them collided, squashing the huge cup of coffee between them. The majority of the drink splashed across Scrawny Guy's chest, but as the cup was knocked from his grasp, some splattered down the mark's jacket.

The mark flinched. "What the..."

"Oh, buddy, I am so sorry." Scrawny Guy pawed at the mark's jacket with a paper napkin, which had come to hand conveniently quickly.

"Charles, I'll have to call you back." The mark hung up while struggling to fend off Scrawny Guy with his free hand.

Wiping the jacket with dogged determination, Scrawny Guy said, "Buddy, you dropped this." With his free hand, he offered the hundred dollars. "I was trying to catch you to give it back."

"No, I don't think..." The mark tried to shield himself with one hand, while his other slipped inside his jacket, where he obviously felt the reassuring bulge of his wallet. "Nope. It's not mine."

Still pawing, Scrawny Guy pushed the bill behind the white handkerchief in the mark's breast pocket. "So, take it for dry cleaning. I insist. It's the least I can do after messing up such a fine jacket." He now used both hands to wipe the stain.

"That's very kind." The mark raised both arms to shield himself from the onslaught. "But it's okay now. Really. Thanks."

"Hey, just paying it forward, buddy. As my dear old gramps used to say, 'The Lord don't welcome in the unneighborly, do He?'" Scrawny Guy smiled.

"Your grandpa sounds very wise, but, er, I need to get going." The mark gestured down the street as he backed away.

"Only too happy to help, buddy." Scrawny Guy waved. "You take care now." He turned and scurried up the sidewalk toward the junction, heading for the nearest escape route off Broadway. Unfortunately for him, he was also heading straight toward Tess.

Tess had to admit that the guy was smooth. Great timing – the collision was spot-on. Offering the hundred was a fantastic touch – it didn't just make him seem genuine, but the misdirection stole the mark's attention. And his hands? Like lightning. As pickpockets went, this guy had real skills.

When Sergei Ivanovic had taught Tess the basics of pickpocketing in Shanghai, she'd practiced in the usual places – the subway, the mall, a sports arena. Such places were ideal because a degree of jostling with strangers was so commonplace, people accepted it. Easy pickings.

However, a more audacious pickpocket didn't want to be jostled against just any old Joe, but preferred to initiate contact themselves with a carefully selected mark. It was simple math – a random Joe's wallet might only contain enough cash for a family night out at the local burger joint, whereas the reward from a carefully selected target could be anything from an Amex card with no limit to the keys to a brand-new Lexus.

So what was the prize in this instance?

Tess stepped out in front of Scrawny Guy. "Impressive." She smiled. "Now, hand it over."

He frowned. "Huh?"

"Wallet? Car keys? Watch?" Holding out her open hand, she flicked her fingers back toward her, indicating she wanted him to put whatever he'd taken into her palm.

With a snort of derision, he sidestepped to go around her.

She blocked his path.

He stepped the other way.

Again, she blocked him. "Hand it over. Or do we have a problem here?"

At five feet seven inches, Tess was taller than the average woman, but this guy towered over her. With his lips curled into a snarl and his eyes wide, he leaned down and stared into her face. "Ain't no one got a problem here but you." His breath smelled of stale cigarettes. "Now move. Or I'll move you."

She did not move.

Scrawny Guy's jaw set and his breathing came in snorts. He shot a glance over his shoulder, then glowered at her, beads of sweat forming on his brow. Finally, he stepped to his right to pass her. He obviously wanted to avoid a 'problem' in case a police officer just happened by at the precise moment the mark realized something was missing and connected the dots.

As he sidestepped, Tess matched him to block him still.

His eyes wild, he said in a hushed voice, "You're angling for a slap, bitch."

She locked his gaze. "You're going to give me what you took. Then, to prove just what a good little citizen you are, you're going to pick up that cup and drop it in the trash."

Fury burning in his eyes, he shoved her on the upper arm to knock her aside. But Tess had already spread her feet for a stable stance. She didn't budge.

In a court of law, his action would be deemed an assault. Not that she was remotely interested in anything the law had to offer – if something didn't work, only a fool continued using it.

She cocked an eyebrow at him, her hand still out. "Give it to me. Now."

He shoved her harder. Hard enough that a normal woman would have fallen sideways.

The only way this guy was ever going to learn was the hard way. And when Tess wanted to be, she could be one hell of a teacher. A smirk flickered across her face for a split second, then...

Her hands shot out in a blur of synchronized motion.

She grasped the thumb of his pushing hand and levered it back on itself to lock the joint, thus immobilizing that whole arm. With her other hand, she grabbed his crotch. Clawed her fingers around his junk. Squeezed.

He yelped.

He pulled his free hand back to punch her.

She crushed his junk harder. "I don't think so."

With a breathy squeal, he hunched over. He shrank from towering over her to being a cringing mass of awkward, gangly limbs barely her size.

She said, "The more you struggle, the more I'll squeeze. Got it?"

Through gasped breaths, he said, "Okay. Okay."

"You're sure we're on the same page?"

"Yeah, yeah." He sucked through his teeth in pain. "Just don't squeeze. Please, don't squeeze."

"Show me what you took."

Cringing, he fumbled a set of car keys from his pocket, BMW emblazoned on the fob.

"Now, drop them into my jacket pocket."

He did so.

"Good boy. So, do you want to pick up that cup now?"

"Yeah. Just let go so I can."

Tess snickered. "Yeah, right."

Bending his thumb against the joint and mashing his junk, she marched him backwards along the sidewalk. He grimaced and twisted with every step, but didn't appear to be trying to break free, only to maneuver into a position that might relieve the pain.

A young Latino man talking on his cell phone frowned at Scrawny Guy backpedaling with Tess's hand clutching his groin. He gave them a wide berth, but carried on chatting as he ambled on his way, as if the spectacle was an everyday occurrence.

Exiting a bakery, a gray-haired woman saw Tess and her jaw dropped. She pulled her wheeled basket back into the store.

Some passersby saw the incident, while others were too preoccupied to notice. Of those who saw, not one person said anything. No one wanted to get involved. As Tess knew they wouldn't. It was a fact upon which she relied often.

She stopped beside the discarded cup, which was marked 'Coffee Shack' in big bamboo-style letters. She let go of Scrawny Guy's thumb, then grabbed his chin and twisted his head around, so he looked at the cup.

"So do you want to pick that up?" Tess said.

"Oh God, yeah."

"What's the magic word?"

"What?"

She twisted her hand on his groin, stretching skin that should never be stretched.

Grimacing, he hunched over, trying to pull away from the pain. "Please. Please, let me pick it up. Please."

"There's a good boy." She released him.

He gasped and clutched his groin, doubling up. "Ohhhh, Jesus."

"Hey."

He looked up. Tess nodded to the cup.

Still hunched, he hobbled over to it, sucked through his teeth as he stooped and picked it up, then lurched over to a nearby trash can. However, instead of dropping the cup into the trash, he tossed it on the ground. He flipped Tess the finger, then he turned and ran, barging pedestrians out of his way.

He shot out into the road.

A silver SUV honked at him as it hammered on the brakes. Scrawny Guy didn't even look, but just flew across to the other sidewalk and disappeared into the throng on that side of the street.

Tess sighed. She didn't have time to chase him and it wasn't worth drawing too much attention over something so trivial when she was supposed to be on the trail of a killer. Especially when that traffic camera could capture everything on the sidewalk opposite.

She meandered over to the cup and dropped it in the trash can.

People. What the hell was wrong with them?

Tess left the car keys with a rosy-cheeked receptionist in the Michenner Building, then, instead of making for the subway, she turned off Broadway and headed west toward the Hudson River. She'd walk to Riverside Park, which ran alongside the river, and on up to the church from there. Bound for Harlem, the 1 Train could take her almost right to the church, but she needed time to familiarize herself with the available facts online and for that, she needed a reliable signal, something virtually impossible underground.

Marching down a shady side street of brownstones, she again slipped her phone out of its pouch and then surfed to the website that had many in the black community locking their doors and only venturing out when absolutely necessary: GodsPoolCleaner.com.

What divine wisdom would he be sharing with the masses today?

28

Chapter 04

IN RED GOTHIC-STYLE text against a black background, the Web page read:

I will bring deliverance unto the city of New York.

I will shine the light for our beloved United States of America to follow.

For too long has this evil contaminated our line.

For too long have our protectors lain idle while this scourge polluted everything we hold dear.

I will preserve the integrity of our race, the purity of God's chosen children: we, the white masters.

For I am the Pool Cleaner.

And the gene pool will be cleansed this day.

Tess shook her head. "Just what the world needs – another freaking nutjob."

She clicked back to the website's home page. It listed 118 'teachings'. She clicked the next one: number 65. The same kind of wisdom illuminated her phone's screen.

She'd hoped she wouldn't have to get involved in this. Hoped the police would catch him. Or he'd stop and disappear. Yeah, right. Like life was so easy.

On the sidewalk, behind the yellow crime scene tape, with umpteen TV news crews and endless bloodthirsty busybodies, Tess looked up at the twenty-four-story church tower, one of the tallest in the world. It never failed to impress. Riverside Church being of a gothic design like the churches she'd seen in Europe, she could see why people would want to get married here – it promised the illusion of that perfect day that every little girl dreamed of. Well, almost every little girl.

At the other side of the yellow tape, in front of the church, a black detective with hunched shoulders thanked a woman in a green Gucci dress. He turned and saw Tess. Nodded. Shuffled over.

She smiled. "Hey, Joe."

"Tess," he said, smoothing a hand over his graying hair. The dark bags under his eyes looked like used teabags. "Ain't seen you in a while."

"Not since Allison visited her sister and you booked the honeymoon suite at The Lucky Streak in Atlantic City."

His shoulders hunched even more. "Shhhh!" He looked around, as if he expected all the assembled reporters to be shouting into their cell phones, 'Hold the front page!'

She winked at him. It was important she keep her cop friends on the verge of having a coronary – it made them more cooperative.

But she did actually like this one. She couldn't say that about a lot of those she bedded to get what she needed. Unlike most of them, Joe made an effort and

30

didn't just lie on top of her, grunting and dripping sweat. It wasn't just sex for him: he treated her like a real person and talked to her accordingly. That meant something. So she didn't mind that, at his age, it took him a while to get going. Yes, she liked this old guy. She always moaned that little bit more for Joe.

Gazing up at the tower, Tess said, "Ironic it's this place, huh?"

"Sure is." He frowned. "Wait, what?"

"Race hate here."

His frown didn't disappear.

Tess said, "Some of history's most strident supporters of racial equality have spoken here – Martin Luther King, Desmond Tutu, Mandela."

"Oh, yeah. Ironic."

Yes, Joe was one of the good guys. But bright? That was another story.

She nodded to the crime scene behind him. "So, what we got?"

He huffed. And again looked around for who might be listening.

"Joe, you know you're going to tell me and I know you're going to tell me, so let's just cut the usual preamble, huh?"

He huffed again. Then glanced down at her chest. He rubbed his face and then dragged his gaze back up.

She didn't mind men ogling her. It gave her power and power got her what she wanted. She could never understand why women complained about being objectified. That's what people did with everything: objectified it. That was the way of the world. Over a person's lifetime, they met very few people they knew intimately enough to appreciate not as objects but as

31

people, as living entities with needs and dreams just like themselves. It was why there were two billion people around the globe starving – they were objects. And objects didn't matter, so it didn't matter if they suffered.

That was the reason for all these people being gathered at this church – some sicko with a rifle had seen an object, not a person, and so believed they could do whatever they liked to it.

Yes, it was easy to destroy an object. So easy. But a real person? That was a totally different ballgame that few people had the heart to play.

She touched Joe's arm and lowered her voice. "Okay, let's make this easy. Is it the same MO as the Pool Cleaner?"

Joe looked at her for a moment, then nodded.

"White male; black female?"

"Yeah."

"No shell casings. No prints. No DNA."

He shook his head.

"No connection to the other victims."

"Nothing's grabbed us."

She said, "We got anything on where the shot was taken from?"

He scratched his head and gazed away, obviously uncomfortable at sharing more.

Tess said, "TruClean Laundromat on West 127th – there's a meth lab in the basement." Joe was Homicide, not Narcotics, so the information wasn't of use to him directly, but, as with every other area of life, people doing favors for each other greased the cogs that made the world turn. He could pass the info on and someone would owe him. Big time.

32

Joe nodded to Riverside Park across from the church. "We're sweeping it right now. And canvassing for witnesses. But my money's on Grant's Tomb."

Over to her far left, a white conical-shaped roof supported on granite columns rose above the treetops. She said, "You think someone climbed on the roof?"

"The angle of trajectory suggests the shooter was up high." He looked away to the tomb. "It's a harder shot, but less conspicuous than climbing one of these here trees." Joe pointed to the trees just across the street.

Tess said, "Anyone see anything?"

"Like we'd be so lucky."

"How about the weapon? Ballistics reveal anything from his earlier victims?"

He shook his head. "All we've got for sure is he uses hollow points."

Hollow point bullets had a deep dimple in the tip which made them expand or fragment on impact, so causing far more tissue damage than ordinary bullets. She said, "Hollow points, huh?"

"That's one funeral sure as hell ain't gonna be open casket."

She scribbled details in her tiny notebook and then looked up at the trees in the park. Their barely budding branches were still. With no wind and using a good telescoping lens, it would've been a hard shot but far from impossible – for an experienced marksman. That could be a useful clue in itself. Except in a city of eight million, there'd be a lot of marksmen – military, police, hunters, sports shooters, gun enthusiasts.

She said, "There's nothing the rifling on the slugs can tell us?"

"Not according to our tech guys. Too much deformation." He looked back toward the tomb. "But for this distance, my money would be on a bolt action of some sort."

Joe was probably right: a trained shooter, especially a sniper, would likely use a bolt action for such a shot. That kind of rifle was more reliable because it had fewer moving parts, plus many would argue, it was more accurate for long distance shooting.

She pointed to the distraught wedding guests, some milling about, some huddled together in tears, some being interviewed by police. "And so far there's no connection to the other victims?"

He huffed. "We've found zip. Just like between first two vics. No one knows anybody. And believe me, we dug deep on those. After how that turned out, I don't expect we'll find anything here that's gonna buck that trend anytime soon."

"What about today's victim?"

"Angelique Marley. Sorry – as of ten fifty today, Angelique Hawthorne. Twenty-two. Got a nice rap sheet, but it's all petty stuff. Nothing that would see her deserving this."

"The groom?"

"Christian Edward Hawthorne. Marketing director for HawShip. Third-generation logistics company with a fleet of..." He checked his notes. "Seventy-eight vehicles."

"So money."

"Angelique wouldn't have ever had to shoplift again, that's for sure."

"Priors?"

"Zip," said Joe. "But whether that's on account of good character or a good father pulling the strings when need be is anyone's guess."

"And we're not looking to hang this on anyone but the Pool Cleaner?"

"Not unless you know something we don't."

"So there're no crazy exes we should be looking at?"

"I doubt it," said Joe. "The bride's ex is deceased. Seven months now. And before you ask, I checked – there were no suspicious circumstances. As for Christian" – Joe pointed to a woman in a pink outfit showing off all of her tight twenty-year-old curves – "that there's his most recent. According to the family, they were still the best of friends and she couldn't have been happier he'd met someone."

Tess scribbled notes in her little pad. "I take it she was the one who broke it off."

He nodded. "A week later, he met Angelique. That was just over a year ago."

"They only met a year ago and here they were getting married?"

"Wasn't supposed to be till next year, but there was a cancellation and HawShip made a sizable donation to the tower restoration fund." He sighed. "Angelique must've thought she'd hit the jackpot – a whirlwind romance with a rich guy wanting to whisk her away from the projects to a life of luxury." He shrugged. "But when your time's up…"

"Then we best make the most of it." Tess put away her notebook. "Let's not leave it too long to get together again, eh?"

He rubbed his hand over his face and winced. "The, er, end of the month, Allison's going into Mercy General for a small procedure."

Tess knew she should feel guilty about bedding a woman's husband while she was undergoing surgery. However, sex was a tool that got Tess the vital information she needed to take scum off the streets. She was sure if Allison was aware of the good it did, she'd turn a blind eye.

Tess smiled. "Yeah, let's do that."

Joe beamed. "Great."

Tess said goodbye and dawdled by the church, passing the bloody steps. The horror wasn't in the scene of the crime, but in the deed itself. A glimpse at the church entrance was enough – there was no need to stand gawking at it like all the *innocent* bystanders, reveling in someone else's misery.

As for the media? Hell, she sometimes cringed at being one of them. At least being freelance, she could usually write about what she wanted, when she wanted. Usually, but not always. Just like everyone else, she had to make a living.

She crossed Riverside Drive and passed a couple of uniformed officers talking to a fat guy with a brown dachshund. The guy seemed more interested in gawking at the spectacle outside the church – from a safe distance – than answering questions. Typical.

Tess had her own questions and the answers most certainly wouldn't come from busybodies who had nothing better to do than stick their noses into other people's misery. She headed straight toward Grant's Tomb, a giant brick of gray granite with a row of six columns guarding the entrance. Knowing if a shot was possible or not from the tomb could provide valuable insight into the killer, so she wanted to check it out up close.

Strolling along the tree-lined avenue, Tess gazed up at the tomb's second level, where a ring of granite columns supported a conical roof. With its plethora of columns, and its square base counterposed by a circular top, the tomb looked like a modern take on an ancient Greek temple.

Climbing the steps toward the mausoleum's open doorway visible between the two middle columns, Tess stopped and looked back the way she'd come.

It was an acute angle, but using a telescopic sight, a skilled marksman could comfortably hit someone standing outside the church. Especially from the tomb's roof, which would eliminate many of the problems created by the trees and traffic, not to mention witnesses.

Yes, if she were going to make such a shot, this could well be where she'd take it from. Probably from the tomb's right-hand side to widen the angle as much as possible and make the shot a little easier.

Ignoring the entrance, Tess made for the second column along from the tomb's right-hand side. She took a photo of the church with her phone to send to Bomb. The second column being roughly in-line with the best rooftop vantage points, Bomb's software could analyze the range and angles to help them get a handle on the weaponry used.

Behind her, a deep male voice said, "Excuse me, miss."

Chapter 05

HOLDING UP A detective's shield, a guy with a wedge of black hair strode from between the columns and headed toward Tess. Probably a few years older than she was – maybe thirty or so – he projected a strong demeanor, not because of his badge, but because of his square-jawed ruggedness and wide shoulders. If he was single, she'd bet he rarely went home alone after a night on the town.

He said, "Detective Josh Hardy."

"As in Stan and Ollie?"

He frowned. "As in law enforcement officer."

One of her favorite childhood memories was the Sunday mornings she'd curled up in her grandpa's lap and they'd chuckled together at his VHS collection of Laurel and Hardy getting up to mischief. She'd trade everything she owned to hear her grandpa laugh just one last time at those lovable buffoons struggling up an endless flight of steps with a piano.

With Stan and Ollie being as big a part of American culture as apple pie, this detective either had no sense of humor or had suffered an even more impoverished childhood than she had and thus didn't have a clue who she was referencing. Still, it was best not to aggravate a cop during a homicide investigation. Especially one who might have information she needed.

So, if being playful wouldn't work, what would?

Well, if it sounded sincere, an apology always gave the other person a sense of self-worth. Plus, the act of offering one being submissive, it could get you a long way toward coaxing what you wanted out of them.

"Oh, I'm sorry. Me and my big mouth." She smiled like a timid schoolgirl caught copying a classmate's work in homeroom. "How can I help?"

His slate-blue eyes drilled into her. "Have you been in this vicinity long, please?"

She said, "No. Why?"

"So you haven't seen anyone acting suspiciously? Maybe around the tomb in particular?" He gestured to the building as if she might have forgotten where she was.

Again, she said, "No. Why?"

And again, he ignored her question, giving away no information. Instead, he said something she hadn't expected. "So can I ask why you're taking photos of an active crime scene from this angle?"

That was a very telling question. 'From this angle'. He wasn't so much interested in why she was taking a photograph, but why she was taking one from this precise spot. He obviously thought this was the prime location for a sniper to hide too.

Most cops got twitchy when confronted by a journalist – no matter how honest or well-meaning a cop's comment, a ruthless journalist could always twist things to spice up a story. Playing dumb often proved a more productive option, not least because it had a number of advantages. Firstly, it made the person you were interacting with underestimate you, which gave you an instant advantage.

Clutching her mouth, she faked a gasp. "That's a crime scene? Oh, Lord, I'm so sorry. I didn't mean to do anything wrong. With all the TV news crews, I thought it was a celebrity wedding or something."

"That's okay, miss. No harm done. So are you sure you haven't seen anyone acting suspiciously? It might not have registered at the time, but in hindsight, perhaps you saw someone or something that was out of place?"

She continued her game. "No. Well, I wasn't looking for anything like that, was I? Like I said, I thought it was a celebrity wedding – I was just about to wander over for a quick snoop."

She held his gaze with the innocent expression of someone asking for nothing more meaningful than their morning espresso. "So what's happened? Has someone been shot?"

"What makes you think someone has been shot?"

The second main benefit to playing dumb was it gave you the option to switch things around in a heartbeat to catch the other person off guard. Maybe suddenly switching from dumb busybody to insightful onlooker would momentarily throw the detective enough for him to let slip something he otherwise wouldn't.

Tess said, "Er... the TV news, the police cruisers, you asking me if I've seen anyone suspicious. You don't get all that because someone's snatched the collection plate. So have you found something that suggests the shot came from over here?"

She didn't expect him to say 'yes' and show her rifle shell casings he'd found, but stumbling over his answer, or adopting uncomfortable body language would do very nicely as confirmation it was more than a mere speculation that this was from where the killer had struck.

After a moment, in an even tone, and without averting his eyes, or rubbing his face, or any of the other telltale tics she watched for when questioning someone, he said, "Why would you think this was the location of the shooter?"

Okay, so he was obviously more than just a beefcake with a badge. Answering a question with a question and considering his response instead of just blurting out the first thing that came to mind were excellent ways to avoid giving away information.

She said, "Well, a smart cop wouldn't be standing here asking passersby questions if he didn't think this was an important location."

He frowned at her, as if studying her to work out whether she were playing *him* for the fool or whether *she* were the fool who, by pure chance, had stumbled upon a pertinent question.

He said, "Miss, I'm going to need to take your name, please."

There was nothing to be gained from playing hardball, and no matter how much she pushed, this guy wasn't going to bite.

"Tess Williams." She smiled and held out her hand.

He did not shake it. "Can I see some ID, please?"

She slung her black backpack off her shoulder and retrieved her genuine driver's license.

He studied it, then wrote her name in his notebook.

"Well, Miss Williams, I suggest you leave the detective work to the detectives and go enjoy the rest of your weekend somewhere else."

Yes, maybe she could arrange some flowers, or sew a quilt. Pompous dick.

Despite the insult screaming to be voiced, as she backed away she said, "Oh, I will. I will. Thank you."

Over her shoulder as she descended the steps, she added. "And good luck finding whoever did it." Not that Detective Josh 'Pompous Dick' Hardy ever would find the killer, if she got there first.

At the bottom of the steps, she meandered around to the side of the building. A quick glance back confirmed Detective Hardy was not in hot pursuit.

Partly encircling the tomb lay concrete benches decorated with tiny colored tiles that formed pictures. She sat on a seat on which a seahorse and multicolored fish were swimming across the backrest.

With the traffic noise almost quiet enough to be overshadowed by the tweeting of birds, Tess leaned back to relax and consider the fresh information she'd gleaned since coming to Morningside Heights.

With a thick New Jersey drawl, a male voice said, "And here you'll find our mosaic benches, inspired by the Spanish modernist Antoni Gaudi."

Tess glanced over.

Walking toward her, a park ranger touched the brim of his hat. A handful of tourists trailed behind him.

She nodded to him.

The ranger continued, "Their construction completed in 1968..."

Tess stood and walked away. She needed to concentrate, so the fewer distractions the better.

Meandering through the trees into Riverside Park, she recalled how excited her cop friend Mac had been when showing her the very spot upon which the climatic

shootout had taken place in his favorite film of all time –
Death Wish. When she'd admitted she hadn't seen it,
he'd insisted on lending her a DVD.

Mac having piqued her curiosity, she'd watched
the film. The premise of a vigilante stalking muggers so
he could blast the hell out of them seemed a little
extreme. Even for Hollywood. Break a thief's legs by all
means, but shoot them over petty theft? Hell, the things
scriptwriters expected viewers to swallow.

Still, the streets were more violent back in the 70s
and 80s. Mac being old school – a young cop when the
movie franchise was at its peak – maybe it made some
kind of sense.

Placing a small mat from her backpack on the cold,
damp ground, she sat cross-legged against the trunk of an
oak tree. Hidden from view, she could use her phone and
the Internet without being seen or disturbed.

She'd never dealt with someone like the Pool
Cleaner. Someone who killed purely out of hatred. Like a
crusade. Someone like that would be harder to track
down. If he was intelligent, which he appeared to be
despite his Bible-like sermonizing, he'd know how to
cover his tracks, how to disguise what he was doing to
those around him, how to blend into the background to
such a degree that he was all but invisible.

Further, the Pool Cleaner wasn't only smart, but an
experienced shooter. No, not just a shooter, a hunter – he
didn't choose entirely random targets like a mad gunman
in a mall, but he knew how to stalk a particular prey and
how to find the ideal spot from which to take the kill
shot, just as a hunter in a forest used a hide to hunt deer.

His previous shootings having been at night, he
also knew how to shoot from a distance in poor light. He

knew how to clean the scene after him, leaving no fingerprints, no DNA evidence, no scuff marks from footwear or fibers from clothing, nothing. And, though she'd have to check the conditions on those nights, he knew how to take into account weather conditions so the wind wouldn't blow his shots off target.

Yes, he was highly skilled, or highly trained, or damn lucky. Or all three. Whatever combination it was, one thing was for sure: he was highly deadly.

But was he truly as detached as he appeared – seeing other people as mere objects?

Maybe his choice of weapon threw light on facts he didn't want illuminating.

Poison was a coward's weapon because you didn't have to see your victim. A sniper rifle? That was a close second because you could keep your victim so far away it was like they weren't real – little more than shooting targets at a fairground. Maybe the Pool Cleaner didn't use a rifle out of necessity, but to distance himself from his all-too-human targets.

Unfortunately, making educated guesses was the easy part. Now came the hard part – actually unveiling the truth to catch the guy.

He killed every three days. That left absolutely no time for mistakes because the clock was ticking. She needed answers now. So, when you wanted to find a serial killer, where did you start?

Well, there was only one place to start – step one. And step one was...

Chapter 06

UNDER THE TREE, Tess closed her eyes.

She slowed her breathing.

The grooves in the oak's bark pressing against her back; the sparrows in its branches chirping; the sun struggling to fight through its leafy canopy... all melted away.

Much as she did when she was writing – writing for pleasure, not for profit – she let her mind fly. She let images, thoughts, scenarios, dreams, and all manner of fantastical imaginings flow over her. Endless *what if* questions danced through her mind like butterflies, fluttering where they would, resting a moment on a flowering thought, then continuing their haphazard flight. A bystander might call it daydreaming; a writer might call it conversing with their muse; an inventor might call it brainstorming... Tess called it step one of the hunt.

She played with characters and events, twisting and shuffling them in her mind to see which could become reality in the right hands, under the right circumstances.

Whenever she pictured the Pool Cleaner, she couldn't help but picture a man. Was that logical, or merely the result of Hollywood always showing male whackos on the rampage?

Maybe it was a mistake to discount women. But...

She'd read a high proportion of serial killers were men. And at this point, numbers and averages were all she had to go on. Until she found evidence to the contrary, she had to run with it. Still, that did give her an advantage – in an instant, it slashed her number of potential suspects in half. Unfortunately, the fifty percent of New York City's population that was left was not an insubstantial number – four million men. Somehow, she had to get that figure down.

But how?

With a preliminary course of action planned, she opened her eyes.

She slipped her tablet from its pouch. RF shielded like her phone's, the pouch stopped anyone from tracking her through the device, or cloning it to access her highly sensitive files.

To start her iris recognition software, she clicked on the file labeled 'Dental Schedule'. That being the most boring title she could think of, she hoped if ever she lost her tablet, anyone finding it would think such an app too boring to investigate. She photographed her eye to unlock all the tablet's features and confidential files, and then fired up Tor – software which enabled her to surf the web in almost total anonymity by encrypting the data stream and bouncing it through countless relays.

People would probably think such a process a pointless, laborious rigmarole, yet those same people wouldn't hesitate to 'waste' valuable seconds looking both ways before crossing the street. This particular 'pointless, laborious rigmarole' didn't only protect her tablet; it protected her life.

Using the fake NYPD profile Bomb had created for her and inserted into all the necessary databases, she logged into the National Crime Information Center (NCIC) website. Containing endless records, the NCIC was a one-stop shop for information on crimes and criminals. During a traffic stop, when a law enforcement officer took a driver's license back to his cruiser, it was to search the NCIC files for outstanding warrants on that driver, or to see if that vehicle had been stolen. It was that fast, that easy to verify information. But what you did with that information – that was where the magic lay.

Tess clicked through to the Gun File, which contained information on stolen and lost weapons. She input what criteria she could, hit search, and downloaded the results.

She then repeated the process with the National Instant Criminal Background Check System Denied Transaction File. The results provided a list of everyone in the area who'd tried to purchase a firearm but had been denied that constitutional right because a background check had revealed something unsavory about their mental history or criminal past.

Searches on the Violent Person File and Wanted Persons File followed.

By comparing all these results, maybe with other data yet to be unearthed, she hoped a list of potential suspects would emerge. The police had probably done something similar already. Unfortunately for Angelique Hawthorne, that had gotten them absolutely nowhere.

But that was not entirely their fault.

Tied to the law as they were, the police had neither the access to the resources she did, nor the capacity to take action the way she could.

And therein lay the problem with the law – it was almost as good at protecting the innocent as it was at hiding the guilty.

Again using Tor, she uploaded the NCIC files to her and Bomb's darknet, a website so far down in the Deep Web, the part of the Internet most people didn't even know existed, that it would be virtually impossible for the NSA to find, let alone Google.

Finally, having photographed her eye with her phone to unlock all its features, she placed a call.

A man's voice said, "Yo, Tess. Don't tell me – the Pool Cleaner."

"Am I that predictable?"

"I'm only surprised I've had to wait so long for your call."

"So, have you already got something for me, then?"

"I've got squat. Sorry," said Bomb. "Our boy's website is registered and hosted in the Far East, so digging up ownership details is one big no-no. As for tracing him through his IP, it looks like he uses a VPN, or maybe Tor like you, something funky like that. Whatever it is, it makes him virtually invisible."

Tess sighed. She'd hoped the Pool Cleaner's website would be his weakness so they'd be able to trace him through it. Unfortunately, in the same way she and Bomb used Tor so no one could trace them online, so the Pool Cleaner had had the wherewithal to plan a similar safeguard for his online activity.

But then, that was hardly surprising. VPNs – virtual private networks – were so cheap and widely available nowadays they were no longer the preserve solely of hackers, cybercriminals, and cautious government organizations. No, these days, ordinary people subscribed to such services so they could do what they wanted online without someone stealing their personal details through malware on their own computer or through a compromised public Wi-Fi service. Yep, today, with a quality VPN, anyone could be a technological super-spy.

Tess said, "Damnit, I thought getting a lead through his site would be a sure thing. You're positive it's a dead end?"

"I've got a timing algorithm trying to ID user activity and sneak around his encryption when he updates the site. His VPN might be a weak spot, if I can ID it – providers are nowhere near as secure as they like their customers to believe they are. And I've got sniffers on the exit nodes we can access on the million-to-one chance he goes through one of them."

"So there's a chance?"

"There's a chance, but…"

She knew what he was getting at. "But it won't be any time soon. Got you."

She said, "How about a backdoor?"

Whether by accident or design, many websites had alternative access points which bypassed the site's own security protocols. With the right knowledge and tools, hackers could just mosey on in through a site's backdoor.

"SQL injection and Rainbow Tables were both a bust, so we could be looking at the long haul with a brute force crack. I tell you, it's one sweet system he's got.

From what I've seen so far, there's more chance of me winning the Olympic hundred-meter sprint than finding him through his site."

She smiled. It was always refreshing when someone could laugh at their own cruel predicament. It showed not only had they come to terms with their limitations but they were determined to move beyond them. That said, if ever Bomb found a way to climb out of his wheelchair and live a normal life filled with work, love, hobbies... hell, would she be royally screwed.

Tess said, "I've uploaded a few files. Can you run them through your system and see what it spits out? Check correlations for any racially oriented affiliations or crimes. That's a Level Four."

Bomb's bespoke software had advanced heuristic algorithms to cross-reference data and extrapolate possible connections. She didn't know how they worked, but she loved what they did.

"No problem. We got anything new from the scene?" asked Bomb.

Tess sighed again. "There's nothing fresh. The info they've released already will give you enough details for the workups on all the victims and families. Analyze for correlations with the previous hits, but make it all a Level Two only. My source says they hit a brick wall looking for connections, so there's no mileage in going over old ground. This guy's going to hit someone else if no one stops him and so far, he's doing it on a three-day schedule. That's not much time considering how little we've got."

"Level Two . Okay."

"So, what do we know about serial killers? Is there anything to give me a head start?" said Tess, "Are we looking for some freak with a stutter who likes slicing up kittens? Or a silver-tongued George Clooney lookalike that no one would ever suspect?"

"Probably a little of both."

"So just an average joe? Jeez, where are we going to find one of those?"

Bomb said, "Do you want the good news first or the bad news?"

"There's a choice?"

"Like I said, I pulled a few files while I was waiting for your call. Most serials have been abused physically, psychologically, or sexually, which goes a long way to explaining why they torture small animals or find it hard to form relationships and fit in."

"So we're looking for a loser?"

"Ah... See, there's the problem," said Bomb. "Serials are usually either idiots or brains. From the looks of our boy, he's a brain, and brains can develop what they call 'the mask of sanity', which means they can pretty much hide all their psycho weirdness so they're not just accepted by their community but become respected members of it."

Tess blew out a long breath. "Fantastic. So he's going to be hell to find."

"If it was going to be easy, he'd already be in Rikers."

If life was easy, by now, Rikers Island Correctional Facility would have consumed most of Queens with the number of cells it needed to get all the scum off the city's streets.

She sighed. The Pool Cleaner was going to be a nightmare to find. "Okay, so what's the good news?"

"That was the good news."

"What?" She sniggered. "Okay, so hit me with the bad?"

"A lot of serials are your classic Hollywood stereotype – the middle-aged white guy who no one ever looks at twice."

"Meaning we've only got a million plus suspects." Dear God. "So how many can your analysis shave off that?"

"I'm just glancing over your files now," said Bomb. "There's a whole lot of data here. Hmm... It'll take a while, but I figure I can create a manageable list. Though there's no guarantee our boy will be on it."

"Just do what you can, Bomb. Thanks."

"Ciao, Tess."

Tess put her phone away in her pocket, forsaking its shielded pouch – she couldn't risk missing Bomb's updates, even if it put her in jeopardy.

She stared up at the tiny spring buds on the branches wavering in a slight breeze.

When he looked at the world, what did the Pool Cleaner see?

More to the point, what did he want? Celebrity? Accolades? Understanding? Everyone wanted something. What got him off? Did he get a hard-on hearing his name on the news? Did he dream of finding love with some twisted pen pal while sitting on death row? Or did he really believe he was doing God's work?

Who was he? What was he? Why was he doing this?

It was no wonder the media loved him. So much intrigue. So much upon which they could speculate with absolutely no need for evidence. So much they could invent to sell yet another story. It was like their own personal soap opera which only they could write.

And there was no end of experts of all creeds espousing their opinions. Some called him a dysfunctional individual with sociological leanings and xenophobic tendencies who needed treatment. Some called him a flag-waving Nazi who needed burying. Opinion, as ever, was divided.

Whatever you labeled him as didn't matter – that wouldn't stop him. Knowing his motivation, however, would help Tess catch him. But how did you get inside the head of such a screwed-up nutjob?

Tess sprang to her feet. Marched toward the park exit. They were going about this all wrong. The authorities had all this data and the guy was still killing. She was thinking too much like a police detective. It was stifling her. She had to cut loose. She had to think so far outside the box that the box was a mere dot on the horizon. Raw data alone wouldn't stop this guy. She had to hunt the hunter.

When you hunted deer, you ventured into the forest with a rifle, telescopic sight, and camouflage. You moved silently. Stayed upwind. Used a hide. The basic principles were the same no matter what your prey was. So, how would you hunt a serial killer? What should you use as bait? Where was the best place to lure them out into the open for a clean shot?

She had an idea.

It was dangerous.

It was repugnant.

It was illegal.

Yep, it had her name all over it.

Chapter 07

WITH A FINGER up his nose, the weirdo stared at Tess across the subway car. He sported red sweat pants complemented by a blue blazer with leather elbow patches. That said everything.

She glanced at the Hispanic guy two seats along.

His shoulders so wide he took up his own orange plastic seat and half of the ones on either side of it, the guy saw the unwanted attention she was getting, but just looked away. He obviously wanted to melt into the background, so he wouldn't get drawn into anything.

Tess rolled her eyes. Men stared at her. She got that. Attractive women had to put up with it wherever they went. But the strange thing here was, this weirdo wasn't staring at her breasts, not at her legs, not even at her crotch. No, he was staring right into her eyes.

By candlelight, over a glass of wine, that could be very welcome.

Across a sweaty subway car...

In the animal kingdom, staring was a sign of aggression. At a primal level, people knew that too. Those who ignored that fact were either suffering some form of mental disorder or planning a confrontation. Which one was he?

So as not to encourage or enrage the guy, Tess looked away. If he followed her off the train and came within six feet, she'd floor him. Her being pushed under a train was not going to be a filler story on the evening news, sandwiched between the latest Z-list celebrity breakup and a pig that could tell the time. She would not be a crime statistic about which no one cared.

She stared out at Manhattan's buildings flying by and the streets aglow in the late afternoon sun. That was one thing she'd heard surprised tourists comment on – how much of the city's subway was actually above ground.

Gazing at the blur of brick and stone, she wondered if she was doing the right thing. While she didn't like stereotyping, to some degree people had to generalize about every little thing every day of their life. It was how they got through the day. They had to generalize, to make sweeping assumptions, to believe in averages. The law of averages said their bus wouldn't crash. Basic generalizations confirmed the passenger beside them wasn't a maniac with a knife. On reaching their destination, assumptions gave them the confidence to alight in the belief they wouldn't be struck by lightning.

People lived by generalizations, assumptions, and the law of averages. They needed them. If they stopped believing in them, then just to get out of bed in the morning, they'd need a dose of ketamine to overcome their fear of their floor giving way.

People generalized about other people just the same. They had to. She didn't like it, because people had so many depths that initial generalizations were invariably wrong.

Take her. Anyone looking at her would see someone who used cosmetics sparingly; wore decent but cheap clothes; had a toned, muscular physique; often had her head in her ereader; and carried herself confidently, but not arrogantly. Reading those signs, someone might guess she was an educated booklover who kept in shape – maybe a librarian who took Pilates classes in her lunch hour. No one seeing her would ever dream she was a trained killer who stole from her victims to cover her living expenses.

Generalizations often turned out to be wildly inaccurate; however, they were starting points and, as such, were vital. To find the Pool Cleaner, Tess would have to make sweeping generalizations and then narrow the focus as she uncovered more and more information.

So, what generalizations about the Pool Cleaner were most glaring?

Simple. Because he'd only shot black women and wrote of 'white masters', he was a racist. All she had to do was find where neo-Nazis hung out and follow the stench. Luckily, she'd heard of just such a place.

The weirdo with his finger up his nose was still staring directly at her. It was as if he were daring her to confront him. She couldn't risk that. Not in an enclosed space. Couldn't risk exposing herself to interrogation by the authorities over something so meaningless.

She stood up and moved nearer to the second of the four doors in her car. It wasn't her stop, but she wasn't getting off. Instead of leaning against one of the stainless steel poles for balance, she held the overhead horizontal handrail, her arm up and out in his general direction.

Now, if the weirdo made a move and gave her no option, she could slam a hammerfist down on his nose or collarbone in a heartbeat and, unless they were staring right at her, no one would see anything but him dropping to the floor like a brick.

She watched his reflection in the mirror.

The only thing that followed her was his gaze.

The train stopped at the station. People alighted and boarded.

A fat guy in a baseball cap shouldered Tess in the back to move her and give himself more space. She resisted. He glared at her as he waddled around her to a spot more befitting his bulk.

The automated announcement said, "Stand clear of the closing doors, please."

An instant later, the doors closed and the train accelerated out of the station. While underway, Tess didn't look at the weirdo once.

At the next station, Tess again watched people alight and board. This was her stop. She needed to get off. But she couldn't risk the weirdo following her.

She waited.

And waited.

The automated male voice said, "Stand clear of the closing doors, please."

Tess shot off the train, the doors almost snagging her as she sped through them.

The train departing, the weirdo peered out of the window at her as he passed.

While she'd have liked to have smacked the guy for his intimidating behavior, it wasn't worth it. With so many surveillance cameras on public transportation nowadays, she couldn't risk drawing attention to herself –

or her skills – in such a public place. No, she had to be invisible.

On the platform, a black guy with dreadlocks played an acoustic guitar plastered in stickers, making it look like an old suitcase that had traveled the world. She recognized the song: Jimi Hendrix's version of 'Hey Joe'. And a damn good rendition it was too. No surprise – he'd probably had to go through umpteen auditions through the MUNY program to get such a sought-after gig. As she passed, she dropped a couple of dollars into the orange plush-lined interior of his guitar case.

The music following her, she cursed under her breath. She really had to get her bow rehaired. Maybe with Siberian horsehair this time. With a little thick black hair mixed in with the white. Try to get that fuller, darker tone she loved. Have her cello sing once again. She was definitely not buying that languid American crap she had last time. But like everything else, it all came down to money. However, if you wanted quality results, you had to pay for quality tools. As her Grandpa had used to say – get the right tool for the right job and it almost does itself.

She descended the steps and exited the subway. On the sidewalk, the rumble of the train overhead fading into the distance, the traffic noise of city streets returned like a loving cat that always wanted to be purring in your lap.

The right tool. That was it. That was the key she needed. The generalization about racism had set her on the right path, and now the random connections the guitarist had set in motion in her mind had shown her which fork on that path to take.

The Pool Cleaner needed the right tool to do his job – a hunter needed a hunting rifle. The police couldn't identify it from the slugs they had, but that was because they were hoping a mangled bullet would identify the weapon. What if she twisted that on its head? What if she looked for the weapon that could fire that bullet?

The Pool Cleaner was obviously smart, so he'd have gone for a rifle that was commonplace. Something that wouldn't stand out, so it and he would just blend into the scenery. Something like... a Remington 700. That had the power to stop a marauding grizzly bear, yet was so popular no one in the shooting community would think twice about someone owning one.

Plus, not only was it a rifle available from virtually any gun store, but she was sure she'd read it was also one widely used by the military and law enforcement agencies. There must be millions and millions of them across the country. So, if someone wanted to blend in, and wanted a reliable tool which was widely available, that would make a great fit. But could a Remington 700 accommodate a big enough telescoping lens for such a shot?

Okay, so it didn't have to be a Remington, but she was sure her thought process was sound. All she needed was a black market source from which to get firearms – find the weapon, find the man.

Arriving at her destination, she heaved on the heavy black door to *The Star Cross*, a drinking hole known for attracting a particular clientele. If a bar full of neo-Nazis didn't know where to get an illegal firearm, what kind of world was she living in? With her looks and wicked sense of fun, she'd be out with the contact details she needed before she'd downed her first drink.

Oh, yeah, this was going to be easy. What could possibly go wrong?

Chapter 08

THE BARTENDER CAUGHT her eye and pointed a tattooed hand at her beer. Tess waved to decline another drink. *The Star Cross's* clientele weren't quite what she'd expected.

So far.

Okay, she hadn't expected to see a rally like the Third Reich had risen from the grave, but she had expected more than this.

She glanced at the reflection in the mirror behind the bar. Barely legal drinking age, a few kids played pool at the back. An old woman sat muttering to herself at a table on the far left side. On the right and down the middle, an odd assortment of characters sat at scattered tables. Odd, just not odd enough for her needs. Had she picked the wrong place?

Sitting on a stool at the counter, she took a tiny sip of her beer. How long could she nurse a single bottle? She couldn't risk drinking too much in case there was trouble later, because alcohol slowed reflexes and threw out coordination. In a one-on-one fight with an average guy, it would take four or five beers for her to start to struggle, but, if the right drinkers showed up, it wouldn't be a one-on-one, it would be a three- or four-on-one.

The door opened. A short guy with a shaven head strutted in wearing a black vest as if it were July already. In an assortment of colored inks, his chest, arms and hands proudly displayed his hatred for any person not of pure Caucasian ancestry. Tess wondered what profession welcomed a swastika tattooed on either side of a person's throat. This guy was obviously one of life's overachievers.

Fantastic. Just what she'd been hoping for.

Straightening her back, she thrust out her chest. Imprisoned in the tightest black T-shirt in her closet, her boobs all but burst out à la the Incredible Hulk to escape it. Okay, they weren't double Ds. Not even Cs. But cantilevered on her muscled torso as they were – a miraculous feat of natural engineering – she'd yet to find a guy who could resist an offer to maul them.

Strutting toward the bar while eyeing up Tess, the man said, "Bottle and a bourbon, there, Jed, my man."

The bartender said, "You got it, Les."

Tess watched in the mirror behind the bar as Les took a bar stool three down from her. He glanced nonchalantly over at her. She felt his gaze slither over her like a snake feeling its prey before devouring it whole. But she just kept staring ahead as if she hadn't even noticed him enter. This was what she'd been waiting for. This was showtime.

As Jed placed a beer in front of him, Les pointed at him. He spoke loudly so everyone around could hear. And be impressed. "Here, I got a good one for you. This is hilarious." He pronounced it 'he-larious'.

As if it were a routine they often went through, the bartender smiled and leaned forward on his elbows.

Les said, "A dago, a chink, and a nigger walk into a bar—"

Tess burst out laughing. She slapped her hand down on the counter so hard her bottle of beer rattled. Jed and Les looked over.

Les smiled. "You heard that one, huh, sweet thing?"

Grinning, Tess looked over her shoulder at him. "Oh man, yeah. That's a killer." She laughed again. "But I got a better one for you."

Les swiveled towards her on his stool. "The floor's all yours, sweet thing."

"Oh, you're gonna love this one." Tess turned toward him.

Les smiled with anticipation.

Tess chuckled. "Man, this is a good one."

She thrust her chest out even further. Her clinging black T-shirt revealed every curve. While her choice of clothes would be a big help in getting the information she needed, it would be a huge drawback if things backfired because it didn't allow her to wear any of her body armor.

Les said, "Come on, sweet thing. It ain't fair to leave us hanging."

She took a deep breath. "Okay. You ready? Okay... What did the guy with no dick say to the bartender?"

She gestured for Les to respond.

Smiling, he played along. "I don't know. What did the guy with no dick say to the bartender?"

Tess said, "A dago, a chink, and a nigger walk into a bar." She cracked up laughing. Clapped her hand on the bar counter. Wiped away tears.

She glanced at her audience.

Her audience was not entertained. In fact, her audience looked positively pissed. She laughed again. She didn't mean to laugh so hard, but she couldn't help herself – she'd surprised herself with such an original quip and her audience's resultant fury just fueled the hilarity.

Finally settling down, she said, "Don't you get it?"

All but snarling like a dog, Les said, "Oh, I get it." His top lip curled into a sneer. "Now, let's see what you're gonna get?"

His stool scraped on the wooden floor as he stood up, grabbing the bottle of his beer by the neck.

"Whoa." Tess's hands shot up defensively. "Hey, I was joking."

Les stood. His knuckles whitened on the bottle. Beer glugged onto the floor.

Tess said, "Come on, it was just a joke. I didn't mean no offense." She hated people who used double negatives – they always sounded so dumb – but she figured the occasion, and the company, called for one.

"You think it's fun to rip on a stranger?" He glowered at her.

Tess smiled.

"Then don't be a stranger." She patted the stool beside her. "Let me buy you another beer."

Les glanced at her breasts.

She patted the stool again. "Listen, I'm sorry. Okay? Maybe later I can apologize in person to that bad

63

boy." She shot a look to his crotch and then cocked an eyebrow.

Les's scowl split into a grin. "Oh, hell, sweet thing, you're not the only one who can play a mean joke."

He sidled over to her.

Looking at Jed, she pointed to Les's beer. "Same again."

"Now what kind of gentleman would let the lady buy the drinks?" He held up two fingers to Jed for two more bottles of beer.

While Jed was opening the bottles, the main door opened and two guys entered, laughing.

With a long wispy beard to match his long drawn face, one called over. "Yo, Les, my man, that the round you're getting?"

Les gestured for another two beers from Jed.

Ambling over with his friend, a fat guy with 'white power' tattooed around his neck who waddled like an obese duck, the bearded guy, said, "Well, well, well, ain't you a pleasant surprise?" He held his hand out to Tess. "Thomas." He gestured to his friend. "This here's Henry."

Tess shook Thomas's hand.

"Tess." She turned his hand over. "Oh, nice tat."

In blue green ink, a swastika engulfed the back of his hand. "Why, thank you, honey."

Jed placed the beers on the counter and they each took one.

Tess said, "You know, in some parts of the world" – she pointed to his tattoo – "that's a symbol of peace."

"And would that be in the same parts of the world where they eat dog because they don't know their ass from their elbow unless they're taking a shit?"

Tess laughed. "Ah, an educated man, I see." She chinked her bottle on his.

"Guilty as charged." Thomas clinked his bottle against hers in return. "So, what's a little hellcat like you doing with a streak of mean like old Les, here?"

She smiled and hooked her arm around Les's. "Oh, we go way back, don't we, baby." She laughed.

Les stuck his chest out and took a swig of his beer. "We've had a moment or two."

With a leery smile, Thomas nudged Les. "Ohhhh, I bet!"

Tess knew she was a catch. By fawning on a guy and building up his ego, there wasn't much she couldn't get when she wanted it. Unfortunately, sometimes swooning like a demented teenager wasn't enough. Sometimes she wanted so much she needed to pay a higher price. The question was, how high would that price be today?

Chapter 09

OVER HER BEER, Tess eyed the trio, desperately trying to figure which might be the best one to move on. Or which might be the first she'd have to take down.

Probably not wanting to be left out, Henry took a swig of beer and then belched long and loud.

Tess stared at him. It was nice to have a skill. She was amazed he hadn't been snapped up by the MUNY program to entertain subway passengers.

She patted his stomach. "My, you're just all man, aren't you?"

His voice was so deep he must've been able to do a mean Darth Vader impersonation. "You better believe it."

She let her other hand drift from Les's arm down to his butt. She didn't know which one of these she'd have to make a move on, but it was best to keep as many options open as possible, so best not to let Les feel left out.

Thomas said, "So what brings you into the Star Cross, honey? I ain't seen you in here before."

"Well..." She grimaced. "It's kind of embarrassing."

Thomas grinned. "Now that just makes it all the more interesting."

"But it's personal and I don't know you guys."

"Come on, sweet thing," said Les, "we're all friends here."

She looked at him. He must have been curious what he was getting into. Maybe it was time to see if her new friends really were the kind of friends she was searching for.

She leaned in towards them.

Taking the sociological cue, they leaned in toward her.

She lowered her voice. "I need…" She huffed.

"What, honey? What is it you need?" asked Thomas in a lowered voice.

She looked around as if to check no one else was listening. "I need… a gun."

Les threw up his arms as if exasperated and spoke at normal volume. "Oh hell, sweet thing, so where have you been looking? Fifth Avenue? Just hop on a train. Long Island, New Jersey, up state. Take your pick. You'll be falling over gun stores."

"Dixies, Jersey City," said Henry. "Ask for Pete."

"Yeah, about that." She winced. "See, one time when I was out with my girlfriends, this piece of nigger shit just wouldn't stop eyeballing me. So I cut him. I mean what else was I supposed to do? Just let him get away with it?"

Les said, "Hell no."

"I mean, it wasn't deep. Not like it was life-threatening, but just enough to teach him to show a little respect. You know?"

Les clinked her glass. "You done good, girl."

67

She smiled but shrugged off the compliment. "Hell, that was nothing. I mean, next to someone like the Pool Cleaner, it was just childish shit."

Les said, "That guy's a bona fide, blue chip American Hero."

Henry chimed in. "Amen to that, brother."

She raised her glass. "The Pool Cleaner!"

They toasted. "The Pool Cleaner!"

She said, "Hey, the Pool Cleaner might be getting all the headlines, but I bet you boys have a few tales from the trenches, huh?"

A furtive glance shot around the three men. Thomas said, "We've had our moments."

She smiled. "Yeah?"

"Tales for another time, maybe," said Les.

Tess playfully nudged him. "Come on, spill."

Thomas folded his arms, "Meaning no offense, honey, but I've never laid eyes on you before in my life – how do I know you ain't an undercover cop?"

She grabbed Thomas's hand and shoved it against her crotch. "Any time you feel the need to poke around for a wire, baby."

He laughed. "Oh, hell, Les, you got a live one here, buddy."

Les watched. Then put his arm around her and pulled her closer to him.

She yanked Les's face around to her and kissed him. She couldn't alienate him this early in the game. She stuck her tongue in his mouth and licked his like it was covered in chocolate fudge. A feel for what might be to come would bring him around.

She broke away. "Don't worry, baby, I've still got that apology to make." She winked.

Thomas looked uncomfortable. "So, how's all this leave you needing a piece, honey?"

She resumed her story. "Well, wouldn't you just know it – this nigger fuck goes crying to his brother, who – get this – just happens to be a cop, right. Next thing, two pigs show up in a cruiser and lay the blame all on me, like it's all my fault. And the judge was no better."

Thomas said, "A pig for a brother, huh?" He sucked through his teeth. "That's some mighty bad luck there, honey."

Les nodded. "Sure is."

Tess said, "So, long story short, last week my apartment was burglarized and the asshole stole my piece. Now, I can't find nowhere where I can pass the goddamn background check."

Henry laughed. "The background check? That's your problem?"

"Shit, honey," said Thomas, "you know, there are other options."

If there was one thing guys like this loved, it was a dumb woman that made them feel superior. She said, "Yeah? How'd you mean?"

"Well, background checks," said Thomas. "I mean, seriously? Look, *you* know you're a good person, *I* know you're a good person, so why should you be denied your constitutional right to a bear arms to protect yourself?"

"So what are you saying?"

Thomas grinned. "See, sometimes all you need is a friend, is all. Someone who can make a call and get you what's rightfully yours by the law of the land."

"Really? And you can do that?"

Les glared at Thomas, knowing what he didn't – that she was a total stranger who'd just walked in off the street and could really be an undercover cop just as easily as an easy lay.

Les said, "What Thomas means to say, sweet thing, is there are ways to get what you want out of life without always following the law to the letter. But that's something we can discuss another time. What do you say we leave all this serious talk behind and have some fun? Maybe shoot a little pool?"

"On one condition." They all looked at her. "I buy us all another beer, while you rack the balls."

Thomas said, "Tell me, honey, do you have a sister?"

Tess bought another four beers while they sauntered over to one of the four pool tables. As she approached to join them, two bottles in each hand, they all burst out laughing.

"Hey, Did I miss something?"

They all turned and each one looked her up and down as if she was naked with a tattoo on her stomach pointing to her crotch saying 'come 'n' get it, boys'. Talk about having them just where she wanted them.

She picked up a cue. Chalking the tip, she said, "So which one of you bad boys thinks he can take me?" She pursed her lips and gently blew the excess chalk off the tip.

Thomas grabbed a cue lying on the table, but Les slapped his hand down on it.

Les said, "Think it's me and you up first, sweet thing."

No sooner had Les spoken than his cell phone rang. He huffed. Checking the caller ID, he cursed.

"Sorry, I gotta take this." Les leaned the cue against the table and walked away, lifting the phone to his ear.

Tess didn't hear what he said, but thought she heard the name Sondra.

Behind Les's back, Thomas mouthed, 'Wife'.

She smiled at him. "So, Thomas, looks like it's your ass I'm going to be whipping."

He took Les's cue. "Honey, anything you want to do to my ass is fine by me."

She smiled. Would he still be saying that if it came time to kick it?

While Les left the bar to take his call, Tess's break split the pack but potted nothing.

She said, "So, what's all this about getting around the letter of the law by a friend making a call?"

Thomas lined up a shot. Hammered the nine ball into the bottom left pocket. "I'm surprised Les hasn't told you."

Checking the angles, he leaned down and took his next shot, but missed the pot.

Tess leaned down over her cue. She let its strong, straight shaft glide over her bridging hand. Glide as close to her cleavage as possible.

She said, "Les likes to be protective, you know. But sometimes a girl just likes to get her hands dirty."

She slammed the cue ball. It hit the three into the middle right pocket.

Still, leaning over the table, she smiled up at Thomas. "You know what I'm saying?"

"Honey, if I don't, it's only because all the blood has drained from my brain to serve other areas." He grinned. "Do you know what *I'm* saying?"

71

She stood up and ran the cue through her hand a few times. "So you can give me that phone number?"

"Now I never said I'd give you a number. I said I could make a call."

The four ball was an easy pot; the two almost impossible. But the two meant she'd have to bend over the table in front of him and have her butt just inches away from his crotch. She went for the two.

She missed. Purposefully. The last thing she wanted was to beat the guy and get his back up.

She turned round to face him. Looked directly into his eyes. "So what would it take to get the number to do things myself?"

His gaze roamed her body, lingering in all the predictable places, and ending on her breasts.

He said, "Well, as we educated persons say, 'quid pro quo'. This is valuable information. What you got to trade me for it?"

She ran her tongue over her lips. "You prove the number's kosher and you can claim any prize you like."

He grinned. "Any prize?"

Chapter 10

WITH HER HANDS on the wall above the toilet's water tank, Tess moaned one of her most convincing moans. In her huskiest voice, she said, "Oh, yeah, baby. Do me. Do me hard."

The usual grunting and panting came from over her shoulder.

Reaching around from behind her, Thomas pawed at her breasts. Pawed like his hands were in spasm.

His bare flesh slapped repeatedly against her naked butt.

And the wondrous scent of urine wafted up from the white tiled floor where countless men had missed their mark after spending too long in the bar. Yes, the perks of heroism were truly rich and varied.

At least, the condom was hers. She'd ensured that. And ensured that it went on properly.

She smiled thinking of her 'What did the guy with no dick say to the bartender' gag. She'd remember that. Use it again.

Offering a little encouragement to speed things along, she said, "Right there, baby. Oh, yeah. God, you're good."

She tilted her hips backwards, so he had better access. Thomas wasn't exactly gifted down there and had already popped out twice. Each time he had to stick it back in just prolonged this 'pleasure'.

The phone number he'd called on speakerphone outside the toilet stall had seemed kosher – the guy had seemed to know guns; had genuinely wanted to sell; and had said she could phone later to arrange a meet. She could just have taken Thomas's phone by force, but then he would've contacted the seller and warned him about her. She didn't need that hassle.

So here she was. There should be a snapshot of her doing this in the dictionary under the phrase 'taking one for the team'. But it was only sex. It wasn't like it was anything important. Why people apportioned so much importance to who you banged and why constantly astounded her.

She said, "Go on, baby. Give it to me."

His thrusting increased. Deeper. Faster.

Good. It seemed it would be over soon.

No, she couldn't see why so many people got bent out of shape over sex. This? This was just a fuck. Hell, she'd had more intimate back rubs than this.

People had sex for one of only three reasons – to have a child, to have an orgasm, to have the other person give them something. If she had a child after this, she'd drown it. And if she had an orgasm, she'd drown herself. This was a transaction, nothing more.

She remembered an argument she'd overheard in a bar in Bangkok. A white guy with an Australian accent was screaming about betrayal at a Thai girl. She was so far out of his league it was laughable, but he was consumed with fury. Yet through her tears, all the girl kept saying was 'It meant nothing. I only did it for the money.'

The girl couldn't understand why he was so angry, why he saw her infidelity as betrayal. Life was hard over there. Brutal. Women sold sex not to feed their drug habits or designer label fetishes, but to feed their families. In reality, what she'd done wasn't sleazy, but noble. Sex had merely gotten her what she needed.

It was the same the world over. Sex got you stuff. Yet it wasn't a commodity people liked to admit to trading. No, trading sex was dirty. Vulgar. Shameful. But screwing people over for colored bits of paper? Oh, that was to be admired. Something they taught each new generation to aspire to.

Thomas grunted. "Oh yeah. Oh yeah. Oh yeah."

It looked like he was nearly there. About time.

"That's it, baby," said Tess. "Come on."

He kept pumping away.

She could probably have given Thomas some of those colored bits of paper for that phone number. Maybe three or four hundred bucks would've done the job. But no way could she afford so much after blowing the best part of six grand on new IDs to replace the one she'd scrapped this week and the one she'd tentatively penciled in as due to reach its 'use by' date next month.

Okay, maybe – maybe – she could get another few months' safe use out of those IDs. Who knew? But there was no point in putting security protocols in place only to ignore them. The only reason she was freely roaming the city was because she was so careful. If she used an ID too often, someone, somewhere would notice her. Being noticed could cost her far more than six grand.

Yep, wasting money would've been really dumb when she had such an easy alternative. A few more seconds and she'd have that number without it having cost her one cent.

Thomas groped her breasts harder and grunted louder.

Jesus, what the hell was taking so long? Was this guy ever going to finish?

Years of practicing kicking techniques didn't only mean she could break bricks with her feet – she tensed her vaginal muscles. Kegels? Kegels were for amateurs.

Thomas gasped as she gripped him harder. His fingers clawed her boobs, nails sank into her flesh.

She said, "Give it to me, baby. Give it to me now."

She reached between her legs and squeezed his balls.

Thomas thrust hard into her.

He cried out.

His whole body tensed.

A moment later, he went limp. All over.

Holding the condom, she eased away from him. She pulled the condom off him and while pretending to flush it, palmed it – such DNA evidence was absolute gold. She hoisted up her panties and pants.

Dressing himself, he slapped her butt. "You're one good fuck, honey. I'll give you that."

Man, he really knew how to romance a lady. She smiled. "Thanks. Now, that phone number?"

He zipped his jeans. "It's yours, don't you worry. But why rush the party? We're having a good time, aren't we?"

"Yeah, but the trade was my ass for the number, wasn't it? I just want what's mine."

Dressed and standing in the middle of the restroom, he frowned. "Now, don't tell me you're one of those women that's all fun and smiles till she gets a guy, then turns into some nagging bitch who never lets up."

'Gets a guy'? Were they Manhattan's hottest new couple? "Look, you promised me that number."

"Whoa, whoa, whoa, there, woman." He held his hands up before him. "I never, I repeat, *never* used the word 'promise'."

Woman? Had he just called her 'woman'? "So you're not going to give it to me?"

"I won't give it to you, but I know someone who will." He nodded over her shoulder toward the door.

She glanced back.

Too late…

Chapter 11

HENRY GRABBED HER around her waist.

With no real harm done, she merely twisted to break free. She wasn't going to hurt anyone without real cause.

Henry squeezed harder.

Hell, these guys weren't playing.

Smirking, Thomas sidled over. "Relax, honey. We're only partying like you wanted."

"I did you for the phone number. I'm not doing the whole bar."

He unfastened the silver clasp on her black leather belt. "See, I promised the boys – if I got you first, they'd get their turn after. Now, you don't wanna make me out to be a liar, do you, honey?"

Henry licked her ear, slobbering all over it.

She pulled her head away from him. "Look, just let me go now and we'll forget all about this."

Thomas popped the button on the waistband of her pants. "You're gonna do Henry and Les, so why not just spread your legs and enjoy it."

She pushed his hands away. "I said, 'No'."

He slapped her across the face. "And I said 'Yes', you fucking slut. Now, I'm getting sick of your mouth, woman." He leaned right down in her face. "Are we gonna have a problem?"

She'd tried to play nice. But…

"No," she said. "There's no problem."

She head-butted Thomas.

Slammed her knee into his balls.

He staggered back, clutching his face, then sank to the floor.

Gripping both Henry's hands with hers to immobilize them, she flung her head back into his face. Blood splattered as his nose mashed.

The sudden pain a distraction, Henry relaxed his grip around her waist.

She snagged one of his pinkies in each hand.

Bent them back against their joints, almost snapping them clean off.

Henry cried out and released her.

He pulled back, hunched up, hugging his arms to his chest, face twisted.

But he was still standing.

She hammered a kick into his groin too.

His mouth agape, he croaked as he sucked in air. His eyes looked as if they were going to pop out of their sockets like in an old *Tom and Jerry* cartoon.

Stomping on his knee, she crunched through bone.

He toppled over and sprawled over the dirty white tiled floor.

Henry wouldn't be making a fist to hit her or getting up to chase her anytime soon.

She leaned down, patted his pockets, and snatched his phone. An iPhone. Great. That would help cover this month's expenses.

Next, she spun to Thomas. "Phone! Now!"

His hands cupping his nose, blood from his face drenched his chest. He reached a trembling hand for his phone and passed it to her.

She feigned a smile. "Thanks. Let's do this again some time."

She stalked out of the restroom.

In the bar, Les blocked her way. "I hate sloppy thirds. But..." He shrugged.

She pointed at him. "You've got one second to get out of my way."

"Fuck the bitch up, Les." Drenched in blood, Thomas leaned against the restroom doorway.

Les pulled out a switchblade.

Someone grabbed her hair from behind and yanked her backwards. She slammed down onto the bar, sprawling over it on her back. Jed the bartender pinned her down by her arms and smirked down at her.

Smiling too, Les stalked toward her with his knife.

She gripped Jed's arms to anchor herself and then whipped her legs up into the air, splaying them.

She snapped them shut on Jed's head.

Tess still gripping his arms, as he crashed to the floor behind the bar, he dragged her over with him.

She landed on top of him, slamming a knee into him to ensure he didn't get up.

He lay still.

A couple of seconds later, knife at the ready, Les tentatively peeked over the bar to see what was happening.

She smashed a bottle over his head. Glass showered across the countertop as blood burst from Les's scalp.

He sprawled over the bar.

Tess grabbed his knife hand, twisted it, and snapped his arm down over the side of the bar.

It cracked loudly and bent the wrong way.

He screamed and dropped the knife.

Tess vaulted over the bar.

She glared at Thomas, who was still cupping the blood gushing from his nose.

"I'm gonna fucking break you, whore." He snatched a stool and swept it up high with both hands, intending to crash it down on her. He lurched forward.

Her instincts screamed at her to pull away from the danger. To shrink back from the attack. To use distance to avoid being hit. Only then would she be safe.

But her instincts were wrong.

She lunged at him.

Before he had time to smash the stool down onto her, she was on him.

The stool held at bay with one hand, she hammered the other into his throat.

Thomas dropped the stool and clutched his throat, gasping. He looked like a fish gulping air.

He reeled back against the video game machine.

She flowed with him. Her left shin cracked into the side of his right thigh, deadening that leg. Twisting her body into it to generate maximum stopping power, she slammed the heel of her right palm into his jaw.

Whipping her hand straight back, the side of her fist battered his head. Her other elbow smashed into him a split second later.

He slumped against the machine.

She jammed her thumb into his mastoid, the cluster of nerves under his right ear. He squealed.

Her right hand clutched his groin.

Sank her clawed fingers into it.

Thomas shrieked.

He clawed at her hand on his crotch, so she ground her thumb into his mastoid. He clutched at that, so she crushed his junk.

He whined.

She leaned in close. "Think it's fun to rape women? Huh?"

He squealed as she squeezed his junk tighter.

"Think it's okay as long as you don't get caught?"

She jammed her thumb harder into the sensitive nerve cluster on his neck. His face contorted.

"Think it makes you a big man?"

Leaning right in to his face, she said, "As for all this Nazi shit? You've got one thing right – it's wrong to pollute the gene pool."

Kicking both her feet out in front of her alongside the game machine, she fell to the floor on her butt. All the way down, she gripped his crotch, stretching and tearing flesh as she fell. He screamed as she dragged him to the floor by his balls.

She stood, leaving behind a mound of ripped pain sobbing on the floor.

Crumpled in front of the bar, Les pushed away as she approached, his head dripping with blood, right arm bent at an awkward angle.

He held his good arm up to fend her off. He grimaced as she caught it by the fingers, twisted his hand over and bent the fingers back on themselves, locking all the joints from the knuckles to the shoulder.

He spat at her.

She nodded. "Nice. What do you do for an encore?" She levered his arm higher, applying more pressure to his locked joints.

"You fucking whore. I'm going to break your fucking back."

She crouched down to him. She had control of one hand and his other hung useless in his lap. He couldn't hurt her. She picked his phone from his breast pocket.

And then she kissed him on the mouth.

He pulled away. "Crazy bitch!"

Tess smiled. "Ahhh, that's so sweet."

He frowned, his gaze darting around while his mind obviously struggled for answers as to why she was now being affectionate again.

Staring him in the face, she said, "You know, I've sucked a lot of cock. And I mean a *lot*." She smiled and patted his cheek. "Next time you're eating your dinner, or brushing your teeth, or downing a beer, remember that kiss – and imagine how many of those cocks were black."

Les's jaw dropped. Then he retched.

She stood up, keeping a safe lock on his hand so he couldn't grab her.

He tried to kick her but she levered his arm up so pain controlled him. He wailed.

Scowling at her, he said, "You fucking—"

He retched again. He spat on the floor and then turned his head to the side and wiped his tongue on his upper arm. "Fucking nigger-fucking cocksucking whoring fuck—"

She levered up his arm. He gasped.

She smiled again. "Hey, I've got a good one for you. You'll love this one. It's hilarious." She pronounced it 'he-larious'. "Okay, what did the Nazi with no dick say when he walked into the bar?"

She looked at him for an answer.

"Fuck you," he said.

"Oh, come on, Les. Play nice. Okay, I'll give you a clue – it was a metal bar. Now, think about it?"

"You fucking nigger-loving piece of fucking shit."

She grinned. "So, what did the Nazi with no dick say when he walked into the bar?" She stamped on his crotch, crushing it against the hardwood floor.

"Arghhhhh!"

She frowned. "Oh, you've heard it."

She threw his arm aside and turned away, leaving him a blubbering wreck.

These days, few people had little black books listing all the phone numbers for their friends and contacts. Most stuck the numbers in their phones and just forgot about them. Hell, many didn't even know their own number, let alone anyone else's. If she had all their phones, there'd be little chance of them being able to warn the gun dealer she was coming. Especially as they'd have enough to worry about with their injuries.

She glanced at the remaining clientele. They gaped at her.

None made a move to stop her.

None made a move to phone the police.

She made for the door to leave, but having one last glance around, she spotted something that made her stop dead.

Chapter 12

A KID WITH bangs dangling to his nose who'd earlier been playing pool was now sitting at a table. One hand holding a beer, his other pointed his cell phone straight at her. There was no mistaking what he was doing.

Tess didn't want to appear on YouTube. Bomb had hacked accounts before and removed footage of her, but it was wasted effort that could've been put to far more productive use.

She marched over.

Hell, was this kid dumb. Having seen what Tess was capable of, instead of hiding, he just kept on filming her. Until he realized she was coming straight at him. He rammed his phone in his pocket and turned away.

Tess stood before him and held out her hand. "Phone."

The kid turned. "Hmm...?" He stared wide-eyed, as if he didn't know what she was talking about.

She pointed back at Thomas. "That guy's going to need a truss to stop his balls from dragging on the floor when he walks."

One of his friends nudged him. "For fuck's sake, dude!" He gestured for him to hand his phone to Tess.

Glaring from under bangs, he handed Tess his phone.

"If you don't want to end up like those losers" – she gestured to the carnage near the bar – "you might want to consider a new watering hole."

The video footage safe, she headed for the door. She didn't have to worry about fingerprints, witnesses, or DNA: like a gang of Nazis would go running to the police about a little girl having beaten them up. No, she could just wipe this shit hole from her mind.

Time to continue the hunt.

Standing on a subway train, she had time to reflect on what had just happened. She couldn't believe the hassle she'd had. Who'd have thought there'd be so much trouble over screwing a stranger in a toilet stall? What was wrong with people?

All Thomas had had to do was smile, give her the phone number, and get on with his life. Why did everyone always believe they deserved more out of life without doing anything for it? Why couldn't they just be happy with what they had?

That was the problem with dysfunctional sociopaths: you just couldn't trust them. You gave them exactly what they'd asked for, yet still they wanted even more. Hell, and that quack Silberman had had the nerve to say she had sociopathic tendencies. Jesus Christ. Like she was like these assholes.

As for the charlatan's other diagnosis – sexual dysfunction due to a traumatic childhood event. 'A' traumatic childhood event? 'A'?

And all that just because she'd banged a few kids in school to get what she wanted. That didn't mean she was dysfunctional. That meant she was shrewd. That was having another tool in her arsenal to get what she needed. Just like ninety percent of the women in the world. Or did they only fuck men for the pleasure of it? Yeah, right. Pleasure had its place, but women fucked men for what they could get out of the deal: security, kids, a house, fame, compliments, confidence, jewelry, hell, just about anything and everything.

Dysfunctional? She knew what was dysfunctional – a woman who fucked a man but didn't get anything out of it. Now, that... *that* was dysfunctional!

Quacks. Ha! What did they know anyway? They'd said her Grandpa would pull through after the emergency surgery. Had he?

A man near Tess left his seat to leave at the next station. She took it. As she sat, her gaze roaming the car, it dawned on her how negative she was being and that the day's events had obviously taken more of a toll on her than she'd bargained for. She couldn't let anger, or guilt, or shame, or whatever it was, blind her to the needs of the job at hand. Such thoughts would cloud her judgment and make her miss clues. Such thoughts would make her reckless. Such thoughts wouldn't only see her fail; they'd see her killed.

Clarity of mind was where the search for the truth lay. And that came through calmness.

She closed her eyes for a moment. Breathed in for the count of four, held that breath for four and then breathed out for four. She repeated the technique until she felt her anger and frustration fade away, until she felt peace return to her thoughts, until she felt in control of her life again.

The Nazis had given her information on an arms dealer, so her strategy had worked. It sounded like the dealer was only small-time, but that could easily be the route the Pool Cleaner had taken. Alternatively, he may have gone for a higher class of dealer. She needed more options. There had to be other groups of people skilled in the use of weaponry and interested in illegal arms. How could she find them and so find more dealers in the hope one might lead her to the Pool Cleaner?

Chapter 13

AS TESS HEADED up the subway steps for the street, Bomb phoned. It was not good news. With the luck she was having today, now there was a surprise.

"I'm sorry," said Bomb, "but with the search parameters you asked for, the results give us squat, but as soon as I start widening them, we get an avalanche."

"So we need reliable info to tweak the parameters."

"Either that or start fresh."

"With what?"

Bomb said, "Two options: we set whole new parameters, or we come at things from a whole new angle."

Tess considered for a moment. She'd hoped the official information they'd accessed would give them something workable. She'd made some headway, but there was no telling yet if it was in the right direction. Should they continue on the path they were heading or should they go back to the beginning and totally rethink their strategy on who to look for and why?

If they started swapping and changing direction every time they stumbled, they'd never resolve anything. They had to commit and see each option through until they reached a satisfactory conclusion, or until it was obvious that that path wouldn't lead to such.

"For now," said Tess, "I don't think we have any choice but to play the cards we've got. We have to be sure this angle won't pan out before jumping on another one."

"That's what I figured you'd say, but I wanted to run it by you before investing more time."

"How's the workup?"

"Good to go."

"You got a nutshell?" Strolling along the tree-lined sidewalk in the shadow of a row of brownstones, she bent down and picked up a water bottle someone had tossed.

"March 20, Monika Frennais, twenty-eight, secretary. Shot 9:19 p.m. outside La Rosa on Greenwich Street, Tribeca. Had been dating Edward Monk for two and a half years and been engaged for nine months. March 23, Della Igomi, thirty-three, sales clerk. Shot 3:03 a.m. outside The Boom Boom Club on East Thirty-Third Street, Murray Hill. Had been dating Toby Kramer for eight months. No engagement plans. And that brings us to today, March 26, Angelique Marley, twenty-two, waitress. Shot 10:56 a.m. outside Riverside Church, Morningside Heights. Had been dating Christian Hawthorne for thirteen months and been engaged for seven."

"Connections?" She knew this wasn't going to be good news or Bomb would have led with it.

"Social media – we got zip. No messaging, no friending, no retweeting, nothing. All educated in different schools. All lived in different parts of town. As far as I can see, there'd be no reason for Monika and Angelique to have ever shopped at Della's hardware store; no reason for Della and Monika to have ever eaten at Angelique's diner; and no reason for Della and Angelique to have ever had any dealings with Monika's publishing firm."

Tess dropped the discarded bottle in a trashcan sitting at the base of a tree. "And you expanded that to include the immediate families and the boyfriends?"

"Other than the racial mix of the couples, there's nothing to connect the victims or the families. We were right – the shootings are totally unrelated."

"You've checked matches for the victims' star signs, hobbies, affiliations?"

"A complete Level Two, yeah."

She sighed. That was both good and bad. It was good because it meant they were on the right track: the victims were random, so expending resources to investigate them would be a total waste. But it was also bad because it gave no leads to help them find the Pool Cleaner.

She said, "Look, I've got a few ideas I want to think through. I'll get back to you later about them if I think they'll fly. In the meantime, play with whatever parameters you feel might help in analyzing the data and let me know what happens. Thanks, Bomb."

"Will do. Good hunting. Ciao, Tess."

Tess ambled along the street for home. The moon hung a beautiful crescent amid skittering wispy gray clouds. Below it, the traffic honked and growled less, but still snaked angrily through the city.

On the way to a bar or a restaurant, a young couple passed her, arm in arm. So in love they didn't even notice her. She moved to let them by as they gazed into each other's eyes, faces ablaze with joy.

Tess smiled. If only real life could be like that.

She was lucky: she didn't need a partner. She was happy to do her own thing her own way without needing to seek support or to share everything.

Thank God she wasn't one of those people who couldn't function alone, or was desperate for a family. Though why anyone would subject a child to the brutal world their society had built was beyond her. That wasn't creating a life because of love. No, that was creating life to bring something into your own that was lacking.

Hell, that wasn't love. It was selfishness. Pure and simple.

If your life wasn't complete without a kid, there were plenty in Africa and Asia ready and waiting. But people didn't like that. Their life wasn't complete without showering something they'd spawned with Xboxes and cell phones and designer labels and high-end sneakers – heaven forbid they should shower something that didn't have their genes with food and medicine and love. Yep, it was a hell of a world they'd built. A real nice place.

She phoned one of the people that made it such a nice place – her Nazi friends' gun dealer. The earliest meeting he could make was the following evening. That wasn't ideal considering that would be Day 2 of the Pool Cleaner's three-day killing cycle. But she had no choice. She'd just have to pray it paid off and he gave her a strong lead to find the killer before he struck again.

At home, she fed her Japanese fighting fish and watched him gulp food as it sank past him. His long, flowing red fins shimmered as he rose to the surface and gulped a floating scrap.

A partner? A family?

She sat on the floor and watched Fish dine. "We're doing just fine, aren't we, Fish?"

After a few minutes, she fired up her tablet and used Tor to safely download the files Bomb had added to their darknet. She entered her password, so they wouldn't self-destruct, and then browsed, letting her mind conjure all kinds of possible scenarios from the fantastical to the mundane.

While she was committed to her present course, if it led nowhere, she needed other paths to explore.

So far, all the shootings had been random except for the fact that all the victims were black women who'd been dating white men. Could the killer be a civil rights activist who saw those women as betraying their race? The website could be just a decoy to mask his true motive.

Or could it be a twisted white guy who some black girl had dumped so he'd decided to exact punishment from women in similar dating situations?

Both those options were feasible, but... But there was something about the shooting at the wedding that didn't feel right. She couldn't put her finger on it, but her gut feeling just said it was wrong.

That last shooting had been orchestrated to coincide with a carefully planned wedding, whereas the first two were reported to have been of couples simply enjoying a random night out. Tomorrow she'd ask Bomb to raise the workup on the victims and families from a Level 2 to a Level 3, so he dug up more information. There didn't appear to be any connections to link the victims, but maybe that was only because no one had looked deeply enough. Something was off.

"What is it, Fish? What aren't I seeing?"

She gazed at him gliding about his bowl and caught her reflection in the glass.

The circumstances surrounding the last shooting were so different from the first two, it was impossible to categorically state it was the same shooter. Especially when the Pool Cleaner hadn't claimed the kill as his on his website. Who was to say the Riverside shooting wasn't the work of a copycat?

Maybe someone had a beef with the young couple and saw this as the ideal opportunity to get payback while someone else took the fall.

Or maybe it wasn't revenge on the couple, but on their families.

Angelique was a nobody with nothing. But the groom? Christian was money. A shipping company could send goods all over the country. It could transport guns as easily as clothes; drugs as easily as electronics; people as easily as food. A shipping company would not only be a great front for illegal activity but it would provide a terrific infrastructure for the nationwide distribution of illegal goods. Could that be the key?

But if it was, why shoot the bride?

A warning shot across the bow? A kind of *Do as we say or your son will be next*?

That was an interesting angle – if her present line of investigation came to a dead end. There was just something about this shooting that didn't sit well next to the others. She didn't know what. Yet. But she'd find out. Except that meant she would be hunting not one, but two killers – the Pool Cleaner and a copycat. Fantastic!

Her head spinning with possibilities, Tess went to bed just after 11:30 p.m. She needed to rejuvenate tired muscles – there was no telling what brutality she'd face the next day, but more, her mind was a mass of questions zipping from one possible answer to another. Sleep wasn't just restful, it was an opportunity for your subconscious mind to process the day's events. Maybe tomorrow she'd wake with a greater clarity into which direction to take the case and be able to push it to a conclusion.

Before turning in for the night, she showered. Afterward, naked in her bathroom, she took a bottle of white lotion from her medicine cabinet. She put her foot up on the wooden toilet seat and massaged a little of the lotion into her crotch. She laughed.

What a way to spend a Saturday night.

Most twenty-eight-year-old single women were out partying the night away at Manhattan's clubs but where was she? Alone in her apartment, smothering her snatch in anti-crab cream after porking a Nazi in a toilet stall. For a normal woman, that would make her puke; for Tess, it was just business as usual. And what 'business delights' would tomorrow bring?

Chapter 14

IN THE SHARP light of spring, long shadows crept across the park's lawns from the trees hungry for the sun's nourishment. Tiny, tiny buds hinted at the dawning season, their tender greenness almost too shy to show itself through the harsh browns and blacks of winter.

Beneath her favorite willow tree, beside her favorite stretch of the lake, Tess slowly exhaled. Her breath billowed out into the chilly morning air, but she didn't feel the cold.

Tess cocooned in a world of pure meditative thought, coldness was a physical experience that didn't exist in the reality she had created. Cold, heat, hunger, pain... occupy the mind and within reason, each could be held at bay. In India, she'd walked over hot coals to prove the technique.

Tess's breath billowed again.

Ducks quacked as they glided across the ice-smooth waters. In the background, grumbling traffic heralded the start of the new day.

Sitting cross-legged at the foot of her willow tree, she opened her eyes. Meditation having calmed her mind, the brutality of yesterday's shooting and the carnage of the bar were now filed away deep in her mind so the vital details were clear but the raging emotions they elicited were now stilled.

Clarity had returned. Clarity and calmness would see her not just uncover the truth about this job, but survive it. The Pool Cleaner was a trained marksman; there was no telling in what other deadly skills he was trained. When she tracked him down and faced him, she'd need perfect focus if she wasn't to be just another victim, just another feeding frenzy for the media.

Refreshed from sleep and sharp from meditation, Tess strode away from her tree.

No sooner had she left the sanctuary of the lake than she saw Wheezing Guy and Rupert playing on the lawn. The first time she'd seen Rupert, she hadn't been able to stop herself from smiling – she'd never seen a rabbit on a leash before. Her whimsical expression had obviously been the only invitation Wheezing Guy had needed to believe he'd found a potential friend. Whenever they'd met since, he'd tried to engage her in conversation. Every single time. And every single time, he'd failed. But she had to admire his tenacity.

Today wouldn't be his day, either. Today, of all days, she could afford no distractions. Not with what she was carrying.

The street, and the unknown, in sight just ahead, Tess's stomach fluttered. She slung her backpack off her shoulders and hung it reverse style over just one arm, so the pack itself hung over the left side of her chest. She fastened the belt holding up her jeans through the free strap. If anyone tried to grab her pack, they'd get nowhere and have to let go.

Head down, she made for the park gates.

Rupert hopping in her general direction, Wheezing Guy spotted her. He called out, "Hey, Rupert's got a new collar. Do you like tartan?"

It was a surprise to see them so early on a lazy Sunday morning, but they probably liked beating the crowds of dog owners to the park. Understandable. But what wasn't understandable was why, even though he was only ambling alongside a meandering rabbit, Wheezing Guy's breathing was as heavy as if he'd jogged all the way up from Tribeca.

Without breaking her stride, Tess shot him a half-smile, then fixed her gaze on the exit. She gripped her pack. No distractions.

She left the park and headed straight down the steps of the subway station right outside.

Leaning against a square, tiled column on the platform, as far away as possible from those people hardy enough to venture out so early on a Sunday morning, she cradled her backpack. She didn't like carrying these things in public. The open city streets were bad enough, but in an enclosed area, traveling at speed so there was no escape? Hell, that was begging for trouble – if she was stopped by the police for some reason, she'd end up in a cell with no clear way out. She just needed to get where she was going as quickly and as event-free as possible.

The overhead display saying the train would be one minute, she peered down the track for any sign of it. Blackness.

She didn't like being nervous. It was a feeling to which she was unaccustomed. And that worried her. She liked to be in control. She *needed* to be in control. Unusual feelings wrested that control from her. Further, nervousness confused the senses. It made people twitchy, made them distrust sound judgment, made them make mistakes. In life-and-death situations, the tiniest mistake could see the most skilled fighter lying in a pool of blood. If not a casket.

With the whooshing of air through the tunnel, the train pulled into the station. Tess hopped on and took a seat in the middle of the subway car, the optimum position for reaching any of the four doors.

Her blue bench-style seat facing directly across the car, she wiped her sweaty palms on her thighs and then scanned up and down for problem passengers. She prayed the usual subway nutjobs, con artists, thugs, and thieves would have chosen to have a long lie-in this Sunday and weren't out looking for an easy mark who'd partied too hard the previous night to be able to handle them. She couldn't risk trouble. Not here. Not now. Not with what she was carrying.

From the faces blankly gazing back at her, or ignoring her completely, it appeared she was in luck.

But there were many stations between here and her destination. Many, many stations. Who would get on and what would they see when they looked at her? A passenger? Or a target?

An automated male voice said, "Stand clear of the closing doors, please."

The doors closed. The train jolted from a standstill and accelerated out of the station.

It was too late now.

All she could do was sit tight and hope.

Who would get on? She was going to find out.

Chapter 15

SIXTY-EIGHT MINUTES LATER, Tess arrived at her destination. Her fluttering stomach had long since calmed, her sweaty palms long since dried. The various trains she'd caught had rocked back and forth, jolted here and there, but that was as much action as she'd seen. In fact, she'd enjoyed the gentle, rhythmical shunting journey.

Standing at the small information desk in the foyer of A.C. Brown's Shooting Club, she gazed about. Structurally, the place looked like it used to be some sort of warehouse. She ran a hand over the exposed red brick wall: functional, cheap, but stylish.

Behind the desk, Barney, a graying, moustachioed man, pointed to the neat rows of meticulously arranged fliers and brochures along the front of the desk. The information covered shooting events, weaponry stores, and the like.

He said, "Feel free to help yourself."

"Maybe later, thanks."

Though her plan today could take ten minutes or ten hours, every second counted. The Pool Cleaner killed every three days. She had two days left to stop him. Two days. But they didn't have a single good lead.

To save time, she'd downloaded and completed the club's application form already. Now all she needed was to be accepted as a member. She didn't like the idea of blowing $1499 she couldn't afford on membership, but maybe it would encourage her to use the range to keep her shooting skills sharp, even though she hated guns – any damn fool could pull a trigger and blow someone's head off.

But it wasn't just that.

She avoided using firearms whenever possible because she needed to justify to herself what she did. To prove she wasn't a monster. That she was different from those she hunted. And there was only one way she knew of to do that.

For her, hand-to-hand combat had nothing to do with ego, with proving she was the best. No, it had everything to do with deserving the right to life. Just like in the animal kingdom – in a fight to the death, only the strongest survived. And they survived not because of brute strength, but because of their strength of will. People were no different. No matter how skilled a fighter was, if their heart wasn't in a fight against a weaker opponent who was utterly convinced justice was on their side, the skilled fighter could easily lose.

By facing off against someone with just her bare hands, Tess tested herself. But this wasn't just a test of her physical abilities; it was a test of her faith that what she was doing was changing the world for the better. She liked to think that was purely altruistic, but she knew it wasn't – she did it for herself as much as anyone else. In avenging the wronged, she didn't only see justice done;

she gave her life meaning. It was the only thing she was good at. The only thing worth living for. The only thing worth dying for.

Sitting at a computer, Barney brushed his bushy gray moustache as he checked through her membership application form. He nodded at all the places he was supposed to nod. That was good.

"Oh" – he looked up and smiled – "you're wanting the Lifetime Platinum Membership deal?"

She didn't. She wanted a one-day guest pass, but she knew paying for the most expensive level of membership would raise fewer flags regarding her form, plus get her VIP treatment and access to all the club's facilities. More importantly, it would let other members know she had money to blow. She smiled. "Yeah. I've heard great things about this place."

"We aim to please." He went back to studying the form and inputting her details into their computer system.

She looked at the list of rules posted on the wall. *Treat all firearms as if they are loaded. No alcohol allowed on the ranges at any time. Eye and ear protection must be worn whenever shooting.* All the usual stuff.

She'd checked online that this was the most likely venue to find who she was looking for: it was the only shooting range in the area that allowed magnum and jacketed hollow-point rounds. That meant she wouldn't just find the usual bunch of weekend warriors, soccer moms with peashooters, and CEOs with monogrammed cannons, but hardcore gun lovers. Here, she'd find guys who knew guns, lived guns, breathed guns. All she had to do was get one of them to talk.

Without looking up, Barney said, "I'll need your license, please, Miss Richards."

With a confident smile, she gave him her Carry Business License, a permit allowing Meg Richards to carry a concealed weapon in New York State.

Counterfeit banknotes easily got into circulation because few people took the time to study what passed through their hands – they had a glance at their money and if it was the right shape, color, and texture, they believed it was legal tender and treated it accordingly.

Her gun license would pass more than merely a cursory glance – she'd used Stavros for years because he only produced top-quality gear – but a fake was a fake. Just as the smallest irregularity might raise the suspicions of a bank teller and illicit the investigation of a banknote, so a tenacious license inspector might see irregularity in the weight and thickness of the materials, the hue of the ink, or the tactile quality of the plastic.

Being found in possession of a forged banknote would leave you out of pocket, but free to get on with your day. Being caught in possession of a forged gun permit? That was a whole heap of shit.

Tess's heart fluttered. Her legs felt suddenly wobbly. This was make or break. This was where she either got her shot at finding what she was looking for, or had to take out sweet old Barney, grab the security camera footage which had done such a sterling job of capturing her at the information desk, and run from the police, who'd be alerted to her crime and have a full description of her.

Barney studied the license.

Tess studied Barney. A sleeper hold would be best – least fuss, no lasting harm.

"You have your firearm with you?" he said.

She pulled her backpack aside to reveal the left side of her chest and patted her concealed shoulder holster.

"Then welcome to A.C.'s, Miss Richards." He handed her gun license back. Smiled. "You okay for ammo? Our prices are very competitive." He gestured to a display of various boxes of ammo, paper targets and other shooting paraphernalia behind him. Fifty-round boxes of 9mm ammo were $19.95 a pop.

"Hit me with eight boxes of your nine mil and, er" – she scanned the display of targets – "I'll take a pack of those and those. Thanks."

She placed Meg Richards's credit card on the counter and then rooted in her backpack.

Barney picked up the credit card to ring in the transaction.

"Just a sec." Tess took out some money. "I'll pay for the ammo and targets in cash, if that's okay."

"No problem at all, Miss Richards," said Barney, "It's my pleasure."

Before leaving her apartment, she'd checked her credit card balance – this would max it out.

As for her checking account...

She looked at the $67 in her hand which had to last her until the end of the month. What would she manage to spend such a princely sum on? Thank God she had her rent payments already covered.

But there was no use worrying about money. It wasn't like she could do anything about it. Despite the public service she was providing, she didn't think the IRS would take kindly to her claiming all this as expenses against her taxes.

Tess said, "Do you have a list of members, please? It would be nice to see if there's anyone I know."

The Pool Cleaner was an excellent shot, so he had to practice somewhere to keep his skills sharp. A list of members would be an excellent starting point for Bomb to work from.

"Gee, I'm sorry, Miss Richards, but that's against our privacy policy."

"Never mind. I'm sure there're plenty of nice people here. And, please, it's Meg."

Barney tapped the side of his nose and then pointed to a notice board to the right of his desk. "That there lists all the various club teams, their members, and our various activities. You might want to see if anything tickles your fancy."

"Thanks, Barney." He couldn't give her a list of members, but he could point her to the club's most active shooters. For now, that was a decent start. She'd have Bomb hack the club's database later.

Barney gave her a quick tour and then left her in the indoor shooting range, essentially, a concrete bunker hewn out of the old warehouse's basement. She picked the middle shooting station of the fifteen available so she could see and more importantly, be seen. With the show she was going to put on, being seen was vital.

Chapter 16

HANGING ONE OF her Q Targets, a target shaped more like a bottle than a person, she hit the button on the side of her station and the electronic target carrier whisked it away to the far end.

Having completed her stretching exercises to ensure her muscles were relaxed, she put on her ear and eye protectors and then slapped a seventeen-round magazine into her Glock 19 semiautomatic.

She adopted her shooting stance and cleared her mind of all thoughts but herself, her gun, and her target. She inhaled slowly and calmly, lowering her breathing rate, lowering her heart rate.

Her pistol became an extension of her hand.

Her hand reached for the target.

The target became an extension of her mind.

Everything connected. There was no separation.

The iron sights of her Glock locked onto the target in the range and in her mind.

In her mind, she fired and saw the bullet zip through the target, straight and true.

She squeezed the trigger.

Bang!

In reality, the bullet zipped through the target, straight and true.

She took up the slack on the trigger again. She waited for her physiology to be at its minimally active. And...

Bang!

Over the next couple of minutes, seventeen spent shell casings ejected onto the concrete floor as seventeen holes appeared in Tess's target, all grouped in the 'head' area. If it had been a person, their entire face would've been blasted out.

Training to fight essentially involved muscle memory: drilling moves over and over again didn't just make those movements come naturally, but made them come as if of their own accord, as if her limbs had wills of their own. If someone attacked her, she couldn't take a moment to consider which technique to use to block their strike and after that, which technique to use to counterattack. No, if someone attacked her, she didn't have the luxury of time to make decisions and plan moves – she needed an instant response. Muscle memory allowed her body to operate on autopilot, so her hands punched all of their own accord, her legs kicked all without her having to even think about it. It was as if she wasn't even there.

Shooting was different. Practice was important, but the artistry of it came in the subtlest of ways. Learning to shoot between breaths, so your body was still, was easy. Any weekend marksman could tell you that. You moved when you breathed, and steadiness was imperative to accuracy. So shooting between breaths was mere common sense.

107

However, it was old Sergei Ivanovic, ex-Spetsnaz, in Shanghai who'd provided the clue that took her shooting skills to the next level. A clue few could master without supreme body control, but which could deliver devastating results.

Heartbeats.

Her pulse was a tiny jolt that traveled throughout her entire body. A tiny jolt that created tiny movements in every part it passed through. A tiny movement that could knock her aim off target by a fraction of a degree or so. A degree when shooting a close object could mean nothing. A degree at a hundred feet could mean the difference between hitting her target or hitting the innocent bystander next to it. The secret to deadly accuracy wasn't just to shoot between breaths, but between heartbeats. Only then was the body in its most still, most deadly state.

After emptying her magazine, Tess knew what she'd hit on her target. But other people didn't. She pressed the button and the carrier whisked her target back to her. As in any competitive arena, people liked to believe they were doing well, so they were always eager to check out how others were doing in comparison. She wondered how many of the shooters at the other stations were curious, not just about their own performance, but about the performance of a new member. It was human nature. A nature she needed to exploit.

Being in no rush, Tess took her time reloading. She fully expected to be there most of the day, so there was no point in burning through all her ammo for just those people now present. She needed to pace herself. Let those so inclined approach her. Let those eager to welcome another gun nut to the fold seek her out. Let them quiz her so she, in turn, could naturally quiz them without raising any alarms. After all, she was just warming up here. If they wanted a gun nut, hell, was she going to give them one – when they saw her shoot, man, were they going to shoot in their pants.

She pushed the button and watched the target glide back to the far end of the range again. Then she opened up with her pistol.

***

Consisting of a single sheet with nine bull's-eye targets in three rows of three, an NRA B2 target hung at the end of the bunker.

Tess squeezed her trigger.

The top right bull's-eye burst apart.

A succession of shots blasted out the entire center of that target. Just like the three bull's-eyes on the middle row on the same target sheet. And the three on the bottom row. Of the nine distinct bull's-eye targets, only the top left and top center remained intact. The sheet hung in tatters. Yet outside all the bull's-eye target areas, the sheet was utterly pristine.

Her mag empty, Tess removed her ear protectors and pushed the button to retrieve the target.

A voice said, "Darn fine shooting there, Miss, if I may say so."

She turned.

With a check shirt struggling to constrain his pot belly, a man pointed to her target. "I've been shooting forty-eight years, but I'll be darned if I can group like that."

She smiled. "Thank you." She opened her pistol's slide to ensure it was safe, even though she knew it was empty.

His younger friend, a gangly guy with short-cropped ginger hair, squinted at the target as it glided towards them. He nudged his friend. "Holy hell, Ned, there's not a single shot off target." He laughed.

The first man pointed to her gun. "And that there's just a standard Glock? No mods?"

The range was noisy, so Tess spoke loudly. But that wasn't the main reason for the volume – she needed as many people as possible to hear the conversation. Initially, at least.

She said, "Yep, just a standard 19. Four-inch barrel. Seventeen in the mag."

His friend said, "Don't you find it a smidge on the light side?"

She looked down at it lying in her hand. "But that's the beauty of it. Because it's polymer, the mag's staggered." She pointed at his Colt, an old-style revolver using .357 magnum ammo. "Your Peacemaker might have more stopping power, but six shots and you're screwed – I can get thirty-three rounds in this little baby."

The older man held out his hand. "The name's Ned. This here's Peck." He gestured to his friend.

Tess remembered she was in character. "Meg." She shook each of their hands.

Ned rubbed his chin. "If you don't mind me asking, where on God's green earth did you learn to pepper a bull like that? The forces?"

Tess said, "You think that's good, you should see my brother."

Ned nodded. "Ah, don't tell me – your dad."

She smiled. "How'd you guess? Yeah, I could hold a gun before I could hold a knife and fork."

"Good for him. A father should do right by his kids."

Tess snickered. "Tell me about it. Maybe if more did, we wouldn't have all the trouble we got in the world now."

Ned huffed. "You ain't wrong there, Meg."

Peck said, "So what brings you to old A.C.'s?"

"I heard good things about it. Good place; great people."

Ned smiled. "Well, we like to think we do our best. So which club have you moved from?"

Tess ejected her empty magazine. "Actually, I've been working in Asia for a while. Just got back from Thailand and needed some action, you know?"

Ned nodded. "Thailand, huh?"

"Yeah, have you been?"

He laughed. "No, I'm, er, not really a big fan of that neck of the woods. The good old U.S. of A. is plenty big enough for me."

She started filling the magazine by hand. That wasted more time than using a speedloader. "Pity. You'd like it – they've got a great gun culture. I tell you, you can get virtually anything over there. *Anything*. Not like here." She laughed. "Course, that's more with a wink and a nod than licenses and background checks, if you catch my drift."

Ned's eyebrows raised. "Is that right?"

"Oh man, yeah. I had a couple of custom semi-automatic handguns, an AK, even an M4. Course I had to sell everything to move back here. And now what?" She held up her gun. "This is my home defense? *Really?*"

Peck grinned wide-eyed. "An M4, huh?"

111

"Military grade. Laser sights. Flash suppressor. The lot. And, man, what a gun! Everything you've ever dreamed of and more. Aside from the odd stoppage, but, hey, with kit like that, that's no biggie, is it?"

Ned nodded. "Sure does sound a beaut. Pity you had to sell it."

She sighed. "Yeah. I think I miss that the most."

He smiled. "Well, with an aim like yours, who needs a laser-sighted assault rifle?"

Tess laughed.

He waved. "Anyway, we won't keep you from your practice. We just wanted to welcome you to the club, is all."

"Thank you." Tess watched them walk along the back wall behind the shooting stations toward the exit.

Great. Yet another dead-end conversation.

Why were the people here so nice? Where was all the scum? Weren't any of the members survivalist nuts or black-market traders? Hell, right now, a common thief trying to off-load a stolen piece would be a godsend.

She opened another box of the second lot of rounds she'd had to buy. Her eleventh box. Maybe this was all a mistake. Maybe she was following completely the wrong line of investigation. Maybe while she was playing cowboy in this dungeon, the Pool Cleaner was out selecting his next target.

She slapped the full magazine into her pistol and looked up to press the button to send her target down the range again. But, from the corner of her eye, she noticed someone lurking.

"Oh." She smiled. "Hi. Can I help you?"

A middle-aged man with greasy hair flattened to his scalp stared at her. "You the new Platinum member?"

112

How long had he been hovering there?

She held out her hand. "Meg Richards."

He shook her hand. Or more accurately, she shook his – she'd known stroke victims with a stronger grip.

He merely nodded, without giving his name or saying a word.

Strange.

He peered over her shoulder at the grouping of her shots on her target. He then looked back at her. He said nothing. Just stared.

She said, "It's a nice club you've got here."

He nodded.

She smiled. "A friendly little place."

He glanced at her Glock. "You're looking for a new weapon?"

Chapter 17

TESS EYED THE greasy-haired man.

Showtime. Again.

She huffed. "Well, I, er... yeah, but I don't know where I can get what I want." She lowered her voice. "I've got rather an exotic wish list, if you know what I'm saying." She smiled as warmly as she could.

He barely nodded.

She said, "Why? Are you selling something?"

He shook his head. "I don't sell weapons. That'd be illegal."

"Okay..." What a strange little man.

"But I can sometimes help people."

Strange, yes, but maybe this was who she'd been waiting to meet all day. "You mean, you can help people find the weapons they're looking for?"

"There's a finder's fee."

She nodded. "That's fair."

"Got a number?"

"Sure." She handed him one of her Meg Richards business cards. "I really appreciate this."

He pointed to her gun. "Do you mind?"

She did. She didn't like anyone messing with anything she owned. Especially her weaponry.

"Please." She laid it on the small counter upon which she'd piled her ammo, gestured for him to take it, and then stepped back for him to use her station.

He picked up her gun. Barely aimed. Fired. Put it back down.

He crouched to the floor and, using a cloth so he wouldn't touch it with his fingers, picked up the spent casing her gun had just ejected.

"I'll be in touch," he said, before walking away without another word.

What a strange little man. What a strange little incident. And how welcome both of those were. Not least because, despite his personality being as limp as his handshake, he obviously knew what he was doing – he'd taken the shell casing she'd loaded to verify her fingerprints to see if she checked out. That meant two things: firstly, he had connections somewhere to be able to do such a thing; secondly, he was a serious player – or whoever paid him his commission was.

For appearance's sake, she emptied two more magazines and then gathered up her things and left.

Black-market arms was an extremely lucrative market. As such, the authorities actively pursued those involved at all levels. The strange little man was right to be so wary. And he was obviously a smart guy – he'd said nothing during their conversation that a smart lawyer could use as evidence even if she'd been wearing a wire and had recorded every word. But his words didn't matter. It was hers that counted. Had she said the right thing to hook him and get what she wanted?

It was a short uneventful walk to the subway. Tess stopped only long enough to grab a peach, banana and pineapple smoothie to drink on the way.

The train arrived after just a couple of minutes. Tess was thankful because she hadn't found so many hours at the gun club relaxing or fun. In fact, the intense concentration needed to burn through 550 rounds with high accuracy had been absolutely draining.

After her initial misgivings, she'd enjoyed the subway journey here, so now on the train again, she settled back to let the lilting travel gently rock away her stress.

Still conscious of what she was carrying, she tightened her grip on her backpack, which she'd slung in front of her again to hide any bulge the gun caused underneath her jacket. A trained eye might spot the bulge and ask questions she couldn't answer, but she'd be home within the hour. The worst of the day was over. Time to relax.

Oh, hell...

She had the meeting with the Nazi arms dealer later. He sounded small time, but that could be just what she needed. At this point, any relevant information was good information. But would he have learned how she'd treated his loyalty-card-carrying clientele? The last thing she needed now was another pointless fight.

The train traveling above ground and with the passengers too scattered in her car to eavesdrop, she took out her phone.

The train stopped at the next station. People got off. People got on.

"Yo, Tess," said Bomb.

"Hey. I need the membership lists of all the gun clubs in the city filtered through the data we already have. To stay so sharp, the shooter has to practice somewhere. Maybe we'll get lucky."

Bomb started to say something. But she didn't hear it.

"Bomb, I've got to go!"

The train doors slid closed.

Someone had entered her subway car.

Someone she recognized.

Someone she knew would recognize her.

Oh, dear God, no. Not here. Not now!

Chapter 18

HIS EYES LIT up when he spotted Tess. A great white beam split his hollow-cheeked black face. He nudged his two friends. Said something. They all turned and glared at her.

The scrawny guy with the littering problem from the day before scowled at her.

He swaggered over, his two black friends in tow, one a fat guy with as much stubble on his face as on his head, the other with one of his front teeth replaced with a gold one.

It always amazed Tess how brave thugs were when they were in a gang. Alone, ninety-nine percent of them would cry like little schoolgirls if someone stood up to them, but in numbers? In numbers, they believed they were powerful, unstoppable, magnificent. Like a pride of lions. A pack of wolves. A pod of orcas.

She stood. Clenched her fists. Glared at Scrawny Guy, Fatty and Goldie – a gaggle of fuckwits about to learn a valuable lesson.

And then she remembered her gun.

And her fake license.

She couldn't get drawn into any trouble. Not even the tiniest of incidents. Not on a train. If transit police were on board, or if some Good Samaritan phoned the NYPD and officers waited at the next station, she'd be trapped. No hope of escape.

She turned.

Hustled for the door to the next car.

People were in the way. Instead of just barging through, she thought she had time to wriggle between them.

She was wrong.

A hand grabbed her jacket. Yanked her backwards.

She spun. Hooked her left arm under the one pulling her – Fatty's.

She locked it, levering the elbow and shoulder against themselves.

Her right hand gouged Fatty's face. Her fingers sank into the side of his mouth, between his teeth and cheek. She clawed the flesh back.

He wailed.

The other passengers scattered. Faces frozen in horror, in fear.

Tess stood. Defiant.

She shouted at his friends, "Stay back, or he loses half his face!"

Scrawny Guy and Goldie exchanged glances.

They both slunk forward. Scrawny Guy said, "Let him go, bitch."

"Back!" Tess heaved on Fatty's cheek, stretching his skin from his face. The flesh split and blood dripped from his mouth.

He cried out.

His friends scuttled back.

She shuffled forward, pushing Fatty before her as a human shield.

The other passengers gawked with horrified looks. With no one blocking her way now, she shuffled toward the fourth car door, the nearest to her. Her plan was simple: at the next station, she'd block the doorway while shielding herself with Fatty, push him away at the last second before the doors closed, and then jump off and disappear, safe, into the night.

The black guys glowered at her. Every few seconds, she yanked on Fatty's cheek and made him squeal to keep them at bay.

Finally, the train began to slow and moments later, the station platform cruised by.

Tess shouted, "Move away."

They looked at each other.

She clawed her bloody hand deeper into Fatty's flesh. "Move!"

He wailed.

They shuffled farther away from the door.

The train stopped.

Waiting to board, some passengers backed away. Others tried to squeeze on.

Tess shouted. "Use another fucking door!" She tore at Fatty's face. Obligingly he shrieked.

The passengers backtracked and scurried down the platform for an alternative door.

She held Fatty in the doorway.

All she had to do was hold him there till the doors started closing and then push him one way while she jumped the other.

Easy.

Even if he managed to claw his way out, it would be too late for the other two, and a one-on-one with this fat guy would be no problem – she could beat the hell out of him in seconds and vanish into the night. No one would ever catch her with her gun and fake license.

"Come on." She glanced over her shoulder at the open doors, at the platform, at the darkness and escape. "Shut, goddamnit."

Finally, the automated male voice said, "Stand clear of the closing doors, please."

Tess shoved Fatty away while sweeping his feet from under him.

She spun to jump through the doors as he crashed to the car floor. But she'd fastened her backpack to her belt again for security because it contained her spare magazines – and he'd grabbed a strap.

She crashed down on to the floor on top of him.

Scrawny Guy and Goldie pounced.

They dragged her to her feet, pinning her arms.

Fatty clambered up. He pulled the back of his hand over his face, then looked at it smeared in blood.

His breath still stinking of cigarettes, Scrawny Guy leaned into her face. "Not so tough now, huh?"

She couldn't afford to be questioned by the police for assault. That would give them the right to search her. She couldn't run. Couldn't fight. Couldn't do anything except be a victim.

Knowing what was coming, she prepared.

She hardened her stomach muscles.

Scrawny Guy punched her in the gut.

It wasn't a bad shot. But after years of training, her abs were like blocks of wood. All the same, she needed to play along, so doubled over spluttering and gasping for breath. Abuse like this wasn't a problem. This she'd trained for. This she could take. She hoped they'd be happy with her performance.

They weren't.

"Fucking bitch." Fatty grabbed her hair and yanked her off her feet.

The worst place a fight can take place, especially against multiple assailants, is on the ground. It limits movement, limits technique, limits a skilled fighter's options and thus gives an unskilled fighter a better chance. But if one fighter is on the ground, unable to fight, while three stand over them, there can be only one outcome.

On her right side, Tess pulled her knees up to her chest. Her right arm wrapped up over her face and top of her head, her left, bent, hugged the exposed left side of her head. All the most vulnerable spots shielded, she waited for the pain she knew would come.

"Fucking white piece of shit!" Scrawny Guy slammed his foot into her shins, trying to hit her soft belly. His two friends also slammed in kicks.

Heavy kicks and stomps crashed into her legs, arms, hands, and back.

She cried out.

The police would come if she fought back. She couldn't risk an investigation. That left one terrifying option – she curled as small as possible. And prayed it would end soon.

She didn't think any of the other passengers would help. They wouldn't want to get involved. They'd be frightened of being attacked themselves.

Sometimes, it wasn't good to be right – no one rushed to her aid.

And still the kicks rained down.

Tess put her mind somewhere else. Somewhere where there was no pain, no suffering, no cruelty. She thought of her willow tree beside the lake. She smelled the grass. Heard the ducks. Felt the sun warm on her skin. And all the while the kicks thumped and jolted her body.

Finally, Scrawny Guy stopped. He leaned down to her. "I ever see you again, I'll cut your fucking face off!" He spat on her.

She hadn't realized, but the train had stopped again. Probably fearing the police themselves, the three black guys ran out onto the platform and away, hollering and whooping with triumph.

123

Chapter 19

TESS LAY IN a battered heap on the floor. Slammed back into reality, she knew it wouldn't be long before the pain came. As she slowly uncurled, she couldn't yet tell what hurt and what didn't, but as the cocktail of adrenaline and meditation subsided, she soon discovered.

A hand reached down. "Are you okay?"

She looked up into the face of an old man with sagging jowls. She took his hand and pulled, but winced and clutched at her side.

From a few seats away, a woman called, "I've phoned the police."

Fantastic. Just what she was trying to avoid. That meant she'd have to leave the train before anyone arrived to question her. Before she reached anywhere near home.

The old man helped her to a seat. She could breathe okay, but every time she moved, a sharp pain shot through her left side like she'd been stabbed. If it was a punctured lung, she'd be in agony – this was probably nothing more than a cracked rib or two.

The old man said, "You've got some, er..." He pointed to her face.

She pulled out her handkerchief and dabbed her face where it hurt the most. From the stains on the white cotton, it looked like she had a gash over her left eye and a busted lip. Nothing to worry about. She cleaned up as best she could.

As the train pulled into the next station, she hobbled for the door. There was something wrong with her right leg. Pain aside, it kind of worked, but dragged. She prayed it wasn't a torn ligament or a fracture.

"The police should be on their way," said the helpful woman.

Tess ignored her and got off the train. Wincing with each step, she limped toward the exit. She couldn't risk being stopped by the police. Couldn't risk more people being 'helpful'. She had to get away.

Luckily, the station was above ground – no endless steps to climb up. As she hobbled down one step at a time to the street, jolts of pain shot through her body as if she was receiving electric shocks. Halfway down, she gripped the handrail and gasped for breath. She wasn't going to make it home without help.

She unslung her backpack and rummaged inside for her mini medkit. Crammed into a package smaller than a paperback novel, amid tourniquets and dressings, she found the pain relief pills she needed. She popped a couple of Vicodin, though she hated relying on such extreme meds. Trauma pills made to Tang Lung's family recipe were usually her first choice, but extreme situations called for extreme measures. In the state she was in, when it came to choosing a herbal concoction with ingredients such as lovage root, myrrh and ephedra versus a strong narcotic analgesic, there was only one option.

Gasping with each step, she struggled down to the street. Panting, she gazed out at the darkened city streets stretching out before her. Where the devil was she? And how the hell could she get home without leaving any tracks for the police to follow?

Chapter 20

THE PHONE RANG.

And rang and rang and rang.

Under a pastel green comforter in bed, Tess struggled to open her eyes. She pushed to roll over.

Pain savaged her.

She screwed up her face and sucked in a sharp breath through her teeth as she turned to look for her phone on the nightstand. But not only was there no phone, there was no nightstand. What the hell...?

She slumped back on the bed. Grimacing, she sucked in another sharp breath.

A crack snaked across the cream-colored ceiling. There was no crack in her bedroom ceiling. And it was white, not cream. Where the hell was she?

Like gluing together the broken bits of a pot she'd dropped, her fractured thoughts gradually formed a whole.

And the phone rang and rang.

Beta. She was in Beta apartment.

She whimpered as she rolled to the edge of the bed to reach for her backpack. After fumbling inside, she took her phone out only to find the screen smashed and, when she pressed it, it wouldn't turn on. So what was ringing?

With a squeal as pain streaked through her torso, she pushed up. She hobbled across to a thigh-high unit with four drawers in it, clutching her left side all the way. Inside the top drawer, she found her Beta apartment's emergency phone. It was ringing. She answered.

"Hey."

Bomb said, "Tess? Oh, thank God. I've been trying to reach you for ages. Why are you at Beta?"

"I had a problem last night," she gasped as she sat back on the bed.

"What's wrong? What do you need?"

"I'll be okay."

"You don't sound okay."

"Bruises. The odd gash. Maybe a fracture or two. Nothing that won't heal."

Bomb said, "Do you need medical?"

"No. No, really. I'm okay."

"You want me to call back later?"

"Let me call you when I'm a little more together."

"Okay. I'm just relieved you're okay."

Tess smirked. "And not face down in the Hudson?"

"With what you do, you shouldn't joke about that."

"Really, Bomb, thanks, but don't worry. I'm going to be fine."

"Okay. Speak soon. Ciao, Tess."

She replaced her emergency phone and then swapped out the SIM card from her broken one into Beta's backup. This job was costing her a fortune. And, so far, other than the four phones she'd collected after the Nazis encounter, she had nothing she could sell to go towards the costs.

She limped over to her full-length mirror on the far cream-colored wall. It was the only thing hanging on any of the walls throughout Beta. Not that the other aspects of Beta were luxuriant – it had no artwork, no ornaments, no table, dishwasher or computer. Like a house after the removal van had left to relocate the owner, the apartment had nothing that ordinary people would consider as life's essentials.

Tess didn't need decoration. Didn't need furniture. Didn't need appliances. She needed the minimum of functional items. Period.

Of those few people who'd ever seen Alpha apartment – or 'home' as she usually called it – none had failed to comment on the minimalism. She encouraged that view, though it was entirely wrong – she saw no reason to waste her money on filling her life with clutter that would bore her a few years down the line and then cost even more money to replace.

Plus, whenever she had to move, she moved quickly. Possessing nothing made that possible. She couldn't afford to get attached to things. Not even people.

Naked in front of the mirror, she studied her body in the light streaming through the flimsy blue drapes at her window. While for many women a full-length mirror would be vital for checking their appearance, Tess used it to check her stance, to check the line along which she punched, to check her foot placement and hip movement when executing a kick. For Tess, a full-length mirror wasn't just useful; it was literally a matter of life and death. Without a fighting partner, she needed the mirror to avoid falling into sloppy, and potentially deadly, habits.

129

Under her left arm, a bluish-red patch of skin the size of a grapefruit showed where a kick had either badly bruised or fractured a rib. Discolored patches of skin had sprouted all over her arms and legs.

Wincing with each movement, she shuffled around to look over her shoulder at her back – the same kind of patches hung there.

She looked down at her right knee. Tested it by shifting her weight. She grimaced as a pain shot up as if someone had poked her with a cattle prod. That wasn't good. At a push, she could fight one-handed, but she couldn't fight one-legged – she needed to be able to stand, to be able to move.

She'd ice it later and massage in more of her trauma liniment. She'd also have as big a meal as she could face.

People rarely appreciated the importance food played in recovery – most thought medication was the key. Where did they think the fuel to rebuild damaged tissue came from? You piss in a Ferrari, it's going nowhere; put gas in, it'll get you to sixty in three seconds. She needed high-grade fuel to help her heal as quickly as possible. That meant going out – she only stocked the barest essentials in her safe houses – water and canned food.

If she had to go outside, there was little point in staying at Beta. With every movement feeling like someone was slapping her with a shovel, she dressed and left.

Last night, she'd had to drag herself a couple of blocks from the station she'd ended up at, then take a bus in completely the wrong direction to any of her apartments – not an easy feat – before finally taking a cab to Beta. If anyone had reported the incident on the train, the authorities would have had a hard time piecing together what had happened, who it had happened to, and to where that person had disappeared.

On the landing two flights of stairs down from Beta, Tess leaned against the wall, gasping for breath and waiting for the pain in her leg and ribs to subside. There was no way she could manage public transport, so she'd have to hail another taxi – considering the distance, that was more expense she could ill afford.

Dragging her right leg, she struggled out into the daylight and hailed the first cab she saw.

Relief flooded her body as she finally slotted her key into Alpha apartment's door, opened it, and all but fell inside.

Before looking after herself, she limped over to Fish. He was so pleased to see her he gulped water.

She smiled. "Hey, Fish. Did you think I was dead, too?" She sprinkled in a little food. "I'm sorry, buddy."

Pulling off her clothes, she hobbled over to her drawer unit and took out a small dark-colored bottle. Wincing, she lowered herself to sit on the edge of her bed.

Opening the bottle, she slumped. It was almost empty.

"Great." Just when she really needed it. If she'd known, she'd have brought the bottle from Beta that she'd used before going to bed the previous night.

She massaged the last of the die da jiu liniment into the worst of her bruises. Renowned in Chinese martial arts circles, die da jiu not only reduced pain and swelling, but promoted the healing of impact injuries. She'd tried to make her own by steeping herbs in alcohol according to the recipe Tang Lung had given her in Shanghai, but many of the ingredients weren't easily available in the US, so she'd had to use substitutes. Well, they were available in Chinatown, but she was wary of frequenting the place since she'd heard who had relocated there.

Ingredients aside, the best results were achieved with the liniment having been aged a minimum of a year, preferably five, but Tess simply couldn't wait so long. When she'd seen she was getting low, she'd intended to email Tang to send another batch to her P.O. Box. Unfortunately, she'd never got around to it. She wouldn't mind but she'd put umpteen reminders on her phone only to have always been just too busy for those ten seconds it would have taken to fire off that email. Talk about dumb.

Her irritation at her situation and her frustration with herself adding to her problems, she knew there was now only one thing that could help heal her wounds and calm her mind, so she did it.

After gingerly lowering herself to the floor, she sat, put in her earbuds, closed her eyes, and drew a long slow breath.

She hit play on her phone.

Her own voice came through the earbuds. Soft and caressing. It said, "In a few moments, I'm going to count backwards from ten. As I do so, you will picture your lake…"

Through guided self-hypnosis, Tess visualized herself sitting at the foot of her favorite tree, looking out over the lake. Comfortable and calm.

After a few moments, following her voice's instructions, she saw herself stand and slowly walk into the lake. She lay back and let the water buoy her. The water was as warm and inviting as the sky was blue and immense.

Her recording continued, "Gentle waves massage your muscles. Coolness soothes your body. Stillness calms your mind…"

Out on the lake, there was pain and there was she. The two were separate and yet part of the one whole. Like the ocean and the sky.

Guided by her voice, Tess felt her world slowly regain balance as her body regained function.

When she finally drifted to shore and emerged from the healing waters, she opened her eyes. She drew a deep breath. Feeling energized, she stood. Now it was time to figure out what worked and what didn't?

Chapter 21

THE MIND WAS an amazing tool. It could enable a person to soar to undreamed-of heights, or to plummet to unimagined depths – the same mind, the same person. And like the body, the mind needed the right fuel for it to function at its optimum level. When the body was damaged, a properly fueled mind could help it heal quicker, perform better, reach further. Right now, Tess needed all the top-quality mind and body fuel she could manage.

With an athletic grace, not the hobble of a lame old man, Tess glided over to a similar full-length mirror to the one in Beta. She stood casually. The way a person would wait in line at the bank, not how they'd stand ready to pounce in an MMA cage fight.

Slowly, she raised her hands in front of her and grabbed an invisible opponent's head. She pulled the head down while slowly bringing her right knee up towards it. It was one of the first Muay Thai knee techniques Panom had taught her in Ayutthaya. Its simplicity belied its devastating power. She gritted her teeth as her leg let her know there was a problem, but managed to have her knee connect with her invisible target.

She went back to her casual stance – if someone attacked her on the street, she wouldn't have time to prepare and adopt the perfect fighting stance, she'd have to react immediately, from whatever position she happened to be in. It was logical, therefore, to train from the casual, everyday stances in which she found herself most often.

She repeated the head-pull-knee-strike movement, but a little faster. She sucked in air through clenched teeth as pain ripped through her body.

Pain was the body's way of telling you something was wrong and that you should stop doing whatever it was you were doing. Ignoring pain and fighting through it only increased the damage already done and the time it would take to recover. Only a fool ignored pain.

She knew she should stop.

But would the Pool Cleaner stop?

She bumped the action up to one-third of fighting speed and kneed her invisible assailant again.

Arghhh! She doubled up, clutching her ribs.

She gently kneaded her left earlobe between her thumb and forefinger while picturing her lake's soothing waters once again caressing away her agony. Under this posthypnotic suggestion, her pain gradually subsided.

She tried to straighten up, but gasped and clutched her side again.

The mind was a mighty tool, but it couldn't perform miracles. In her condition, there was no way she could twist her body enough to use such moves. How in the name of hell could she ever face the Pool Cleaner?

She had only one day to find him.

One day before he killed again.

One day… and she was crippled.

She'd have to check just what movements she could perform and what she couldn't. Pray she could do enough.

She snickered. Enough? Against a trained killer, what the hell was 'enough'?

As she looked at herself in the mirror, bent forward panting, a thought crossed her mind. These shootings weren't just the random killings of some nut; they were so well executed, they were more like professional hits.

She heaved herself up. She swung a slow right palm heel strike in a circular hooking motion, hitting completely through the invisible assailant's head, and then swung the hand straight back to hammer with the side of her clenched fist. She couldn't twist her hips fully to get all her weight behind the strikes, but that move didn't feel half bad.

Pivoting on the ball of her left foot, she threw a boxing-style left hook. The power coming from the pivot, not a hip twist, the move came easier. That was a modicum of good news.

A professional killer? Could that be the key?

Firstly, the Pool Cleaner was an excellent marksman. How did someone reach such a level? In a private club? In law enforcement? In the military?

She tried the same moves with her other hand, but the strain made her groan and clutch her side again as if her invisible opponent had kicked her in the ribs.

Secondly, the killings had been carried out meticulously – no DNA, no prints, no casings or evidence of any kind left behind. How did someone learn to do that? Not privately. No, you didn't develop skills like that from a book you bought on Amazon. You got special skills like that from special training. Was he CIA? Special Forces? A hitman for the mob? A mercenary?

Tess tried some slow elbow attacks. Swinging her right arm from various angles – up, right to left, left to right, down – she tested which didn't cause too much discomfort. Left to right saw that pain striking back. She practiced the others a little faster.

Thirdly, the first shooting was outside a restaurant. According to media reports, the surviving boyfriend had said they'd gone there on a whim.

Likewise, the boyfriend of the second victim had said they'd gone to the club outside which the shooting had happened just on the spur of the moment. That meant the shooter must have staked out those two areas just on the off chance he'd get a shot at a suitable target.

But the third shooting? You don't just stake out a church on the off-chance a white guy and a black woman will be getting married sometime that day.

No, that last killing was preplanned. Had to be.

Had the Pool Cleaner merely taken an easy option? Or did he have another reason for having shot who he had? Tess had always had a gut feeling that something was wrong about that third killing. What was it that her subconscious could see that her logical mind couldn't?

A low left kick poked out, aimed at her opponent's knee. It had no snap, no power. But the twisting action on her supporting right knee was too much – her knee gave and she crumpled to the brown carpet.

"Goddamn it!" She slapped the floor.

She was intending to go toe-to-toe with a trained assassin yet she could barely stand. If her new line of thinking proved correct, man, was she in deep trouble.

The Pool Cleaner was not an ordinary citizen with a gun and a lucky streak. She was positive of that now. He was trained. But what was he? Mob, spook, or merc? And why had he chosen the targets he'd chosen?

She slumped against the mirror, head leaning on the glass. Her gasping breath created a cloud of condensation.

This wasn't working.

Gentle exercise, hypnosis, and rest could only do so much. Healing started deep within the body and worked outward. Just as a Ferrari couldn't hit sixty miles an hour in just four seconds with low-grade fuel, so the human body couldn't function at its optimum level without quality nutrition. She hobbled over to her kitchen area.

After gathering ingredients from her refrigerator, Tess blended a kale, beet, chard, banana and walnut smoothie to drink while she cooked, adding a splash of aloe vera juice for its tissue-healing properties.

She then put a couple of salmon steaks on a low heat. High in Omega-3 fats and protein rich, salmon was one of her favorite recovery foods. After adding quinoa to long grain rice, she left that to boil and mixed a salad.

While the fish and rice cooked, Tess lowered herself to sit on the floor with her legs out straight and wrapped a warm towel around her injured knee. Once the heat had sunk deep into the joint, she folded a bag of rice so it was like a squashed ball, placed it under the knee and then performed an acupressure massage. She concentrated on two points which particularly helped with pain relief and swelling – Calf's Nose, just below the kneecap and Crooked Spring, on the inside of the knee.

As she massaged, covering as many of the neighboring points as she could for good measure, she mentally catalogued which moves would probably be available to her and which would definitely be beyond her current capabilities.

Her meal ready, she took it over to her couch and delicately lowered herself down, wincing despite the care she took. She bound a bag of frozen peas around her knee with a towel, then tucked into her food.

Like salmon, quinoa was crammed with amino acids, the building blocks of life, which would repair and strengthen her damaged muscles and tissue. Meanwhile, the rice and banana would provide long-term energy release from their carbohydrates, while the salad contained fiber, vitamins, and minerals, and more essentially at that moment, phytonutrients which would further aid her healing.

It was a simple, quick meal, yet it was perfect for an injured athlete desperate to regain lost skills.

Just as she put the last forkful of rice in her mouth, her phone rang. She chewed furiously and swallowed as soon as she could because it was not her phone's normal ringtone. This one was different. Very different. And that signified something very different. Very special.

Thanks to Bomb's wizardry, she knew it was Meg Richards's phone. Like all Tess's Internet phone numbers, this one fed into an online software 'exchange' Bomb had coded before being routed to her personal phone. The call's signal having been bounced around the Internet meant it couldn't easily be traced. Tess had a whole arsenal of such Internet phone numbers for her aliases. It was far easier and cheaper than relying on burners, and didn't leave a money trail like 'anonymous' phone number apps. To be safe, however, she did replace her phone with alarming regularity.

In recent weeks, she'd only given Meg's number to two people. One was Barney. The other was the caller she'd been waiting for – the creepy guy from A.C.'s.

Now, would this call lead to her answers? The right arms dealer could help her track down the Pool Cleaner through his weapon and put an easy end to this job.

Or...

Or they could prove what she'd been fearing – she was going up against someone as expert in killing as she was. Which would it be?

She said, "Hello...?"

Chapter 22

STANDING ON THE curb outside Hamilton's Family Bakery on East Thirteenth Street, Tess gazed across at the steam billowing from a vent in the middle of the road as a car zipped through it. In the dark, she couldn't tell the color of the car. Maybe blue.

With her toes hanging over the curb and gaze fixed dead ahead, as instructed, she'd heard but not seen the few people who'd shuffled by on the sidewalk behind her. She hoped the person she was meeting would be punctual – she didn't like being exposed like this, unable to be fully aware of what was happening around her. Not that she had any choice. She'd postponed the meeting with the Nazi gun dealer but the guy tonight was in another league. If she wanted a meet with him, it had to be now, on his terms.

Another set of footsteps approached. She tensed. Would she have to fight? Would she even see an attack coming to be able to defend herself? If she did see, with her broken body, would she be able to fight back even if the attacker stopped to tie his shoelace?

A deep male voice said, "Meg Richards?"

"Yes?" She started to turn, but a hand rested on her shoulder. Not forcefully, but with enough pressure for her to know turning would not be welcome. A gloved hand passed a pair of wraparound sunglasses over her shoulder. He was obviously used to dealing with people of varying intellects because he felt the need to tell her to put them on – as if there was anything else to do with them.

She put the glasses on only to discover they weren't just sunglasses but glasses with their lenses completely blacked out – she was blind.

She heard a car pull up.

A door opened.

A hand guided her forward. And another pushed her head down.

She reached out with her hands and found the doorway into the car. From its height above the road, she guessed it was some sort of SUV.

Despite having her ribs and right knee strapped, she winced as she climbed in. She hoped it went unnoticed.

Someone inside guided her into the middle of the seat.

Once in, the man from the sidewalk got in and sandwiched her. "Phone."

She handed him her phone. She heard what sounded like him putting it into some sort of solid container which obviously had a lid, because she heard him close it. Probably a shielded box of similar technology to her RF pouch so no one could track her using cell towers.

Through the tiny slit of light beneath the blacked out lenses, she saw movement up and down her body.

She was likely being wanded for surveillance bugs or tracking devices.

Yes, these guys were real pros.

Completely at their mercy, Tess's adrenaline surged as fear gripped her. But she couldn't afford to panic, couldn't afford to let a mistake blow this job, or, at worst, get her blown away. She had to control her nerves.

She focused her mind.

Breathed slowly and deeply.

Let calmness overwhelm fear.

As was obvious by their procedures, these weren't thugs, but businessmen who adopted a professional approach to their operation. Yes, they seemed a very professional outfit. Even if they didn't offer up any decent information, maybe they'd work out as a useful contact for some time in the future.

During the journey, she didn't joke, didn't chat, didn't say a word. There was little point. These guys were pros. They couldn't be bought, couldn't be flattered, couldn't be threatened.

You didn't mess with pros.

Not if you had any plans for the future.

They didn't know her – if she tried anything smartass, it was an even bet whether she'd end up at her destination or in a dumpster with a hole in her temple.

The journey was more than a few minutes, but less than a long time. She could have monitored the way the car turned, and checked the time once they arrived, to guess at where they were, but didn't see the point for what she was trying to do.

Instead, Tess used the imposed solitude to revisit the lake in her mind, to reinforce and enhance the healing work she'd started earlier. It was difficult to drift away in the situation in which she found herself, but once there, the waters soothed like a full day at a health spa.

Strangely, she caught a faint whiff of salt air – she really was near water. It was a distinct smell, but not a strong one. They were obviously waterside. Not so far up the Hudson or the East River that it was fresh water, but not so far out into the bay that it was open ocean.

Minutes later, the car stopped and the engine died.

This was it.

Either answers to her questions or a bullet in the back of the head.

But which would it be?

Despite the visit to her lake having soothed her, Tess was only human – her heart hammered so hard she was sure her fellow passengers would hear it. She drew a long slow breath to calm herself, but the doors opened and a hand grabbed her.

Chapter 23

THOUGH THE HAND was firm on her arm, it wasn't rough as it guided her out of the car.

She tried to alight without wincing again, so gritted her teeth.

A hand snatched her glasses away.

Before her stood a red corrugated steel shipping container. Around her stood more shipping containers. In fact, everywhere she looked, all she could see was shipping containers.

Elena flashed into her mind. Elena and Catalina and... pain. So much pain. Not physical pain – that she'd trained to handle. No, this was something far, far worse – the pain of loss.

Tess needed to purge those images from her thoughts. She couldn't be distracted by what had happened in Gdansk. Not now. Not surrounded by a bunch of pros like these guys. She turned her mind to other things to drive away the memories of Poland. She checked her watch. Without any sort of landmark, it was a tough call where she was, but from the time, the fact they'd taken a bridge, and the direction the car had turned on exiting that bridge, if she had to guess, she'd say it was probably Brooklyn. Maybe Red Hook. But it could really have been any warehousing complex in NYC.

But the 'where' didn't matter; it was the 'who' that did.

She looked to her host.

In a long gray coat with a nap so smooth it was obviously hellishly expensive stood a man with beady eyes behind thick glasses. He nodded. "Miss Richards."

She said, "Hi."

She glanced at the man to either side of her and those to either side of him. They were all twice her weight, mainly in muscle. And each had the tiniest of bulges near the armpit of their black jacket – a weapon in a shoulder holster. Just in case their bulk and handguns weren't enough, the two on either side of her host held machine pistols.

"I hear you're looking for a number of illegal firearms," said the man.

She didn't like being at such a disadvantage. And didn't want to appear too subservient either. "And you are?"

"The man asking the questions."

Okay, so he wanted to play it dark. She liked dark too.

"Yes, I'm interested in weapons. If the price is right."

She saw his eyeline drift to her forehead and the wound she'd concealed under makeup. The bruising she'd been able to mask, but not the swelling or laceration. And if that didn't give the game away, her fat lip certainly did. Would he be concerned for the quality of the clientele he was considering doing business with?

146

"Let's cut to the chase, Miss Richards. I like new clients, but, as I'm sure you'll appreciate, I have to be careful who I entertain as a potential customer. Your prints – they came back clean."

"You make that sound like a problem."

"One could say a little too clean." He folded his arms. "According to our background check, you're a claims adjuster for Lloyd, Lloyd and Masterson, an insurance firm."

"And?"

"And what's a glorified secretary want with a mil-spec M4 assault rifle?"

She held the man's stare. These guys were as professional as it got, which meant treating them with the respect that demanded. She'd hoped she wouldn't have to reveal too much about herself to do that and, even though she'd thought it might be necessary, she'd wanted to avoid playing her ace. Not least because she detested the sight of it and the ghosts from her past it awakened. Unfortunately, it looked like it was going to be the only way she'd be taken seriously.

She said, "I'm assuming you have electronic money transfer."

Her host gestured to the man to his left, who picked up a black reinforced plastic briefcase. He put it on the SUV's hood, opened it, and turned on a high-end laptop with various other electronic gizmos embedded in the sculpted sponge interior.

Tess said, "Give me the People's First Bank in the Cayman Islands."

After a few seconds, he stepped back from the laptop and gestured for her to use it.

She moved across and tapped away at the keys. "This is one of my shell accounts." She logged into her bank account and then waved over the man in the expensive coat to look.

He moseyed over. His eyebrow cocked at the balance: $6,348,292.67.

She was obviously not a secretary.

But neither was she the owner of such a grand sum of money.

Oh, the website looked boring and efficient enough to belong to a financial institution. It was hosted in the Caribbean, with an IP registered to the correct island. And it was fully searchable, had endless tedious pages of information few people would ever want to read, and even had the option to download the previous year's financial report as a PDF. Yes, Bomb's hi-tech wizardry knew few bounds.

The man in the coat turned to her and held out his hand. "Thadius Jones. You may call me Tad."

Without Tad having to say a word, one of his men cranked open the lock on the shipping container directly behind him. The eight-foot-high steel doors squealed open. Tad ushered her in. "Welcome to my showroom."

A series of lights illuminated the inside, revealing an extensive range of weaponry displayed on the inner walls. At the far end, what must have been forty feet away or more, a number of pristine targets hung against sandbags.

Tad gestured to his wares.

Wide-eyed, she gazed up at the weapons. She knew how to handle a handgun, a basic rifle, and even the odd machine gun, but most of these were so far beyond her expertise she didn't even recognize them.

She ran her fingers over one of the barrels of a rail gun – she'd only ever seen these in the movies where a lone guy used one to take out a car, a building, hell, even a small army.

She looked along the rows of weapons: automatic assault weapons, sniper rifles with night vision scopes, grenade launchers... And he called this his 'showroom'? This was probably the most comprehensive illegal arsenal in the state.

As the door squealed closed behind them, Tad banged a hand on the wall. "All fully soundproofed, so you're welcome to try whatever you like. Within reason, of course."

The length, construction, and ventilation of the container obviously prohibited the testing of grenade launchers and the like; otherwise this was an excellent setup.

"Cool." Tess nodded, gazing about the place. "Fully mobile to avoid detection?"

He barely nodded. "I find it pays to never be in one place for too long."

She walked along the rows of guns and stopped at the selection of small machine guns. She picked up an Uzi and tested it for weight and comfort. "Acid washed?"

Tad nodded. "Where appropriate. But you can be sure no one is ever going to be able to trace anything from my inventory."

She put the Uzi back and moved along to the rifles. All this was way too advanced for the Pool Cleaner, way too specialized, too unique. The rifling of the barrels and the caliber of their rounds would provide leads to such weapons and, thereby, to the shooter. He was too smart to use anything like this. He used something far more mundane than anything here. Something Walmart might stock.

No, he didn't shop here. These weapons would be a liability by giving the authorities too big a chance of finding him. While Tad's wares were interesting, and he was, potentially, a useful contact, this was the wrong line of investigation.

Now, how could she extricate herself from this situation without incurring the wrath of a busy man with a hell of a lot of very big guns?

She paused to admire a handheld rocket launcher. "So, say I wanted to place an order?"

"For a new client, it's a fifty percent deposit," said Tad, "with the balance on delivery. Depending on the particulars of the order, that's two to seventy-two hours."

"And if I wanted something special, fast?"

"Anything's doable. For a price."

She nodded.

One day, she might need some of this gear. This meeting wasn't what she'd hoped for, but it had delivered options she'd no idea were available to her. That said, there was no harm in checking for a Pool Cleaner connection.

Tess said, "Say I wanted a hunting rifle. Nothing fancy. What would you suggest?"

"A gun store."

"And if I wanted it off the books?"

"A guy burglarizes a house. He steals a hunting rifle. What's he gonna do? Put it up on eBay? Or sell it out of his trunk behind his local bar?"

She pointed to the sniper rifles. "Have you sold any of these recently?"

"No." He shuffled his feet and huffed.

He wanted new clients, but obviously thought she was wasting his time. She wanted to keep this guy hooked.

She walked over to him, to make things a little more personal. "Here's what I'm going to do, Tad. I'm going to give you five grand now."

"For...?"

"For nothing. Call it a gesture of good faith. If I place an order at some point in the future, you can knock the cost off it. And if I don't place an order, it's five grand for your time tonight. Fair?"

"I can live with that." Tad gestured to his man with the computer to boot it up again.

She smiled. "Great." She wouldn't lose her money because at some point, she probably would need something. Plus, it made one hell of a good impression with a contact who could prove invaluable.

He said, "Have you got any sort of time frame for this potential order?"

Time frame.

The word stole her mind away.

Lost in thought, she drifted.

Far away from the container, the dock, Brooklyn. But to where? And why?

Tad must have seen her glaze over. "Is there a problem?"

"Oh... Sorry. No, it's fine." But it wasn't. Something was bugging her and she didn't know what or why. But that would have to wait. She stood at the laptop again. This time, she logged into a bank in the Cooke Islands. This time, she didn't let Tad see the balance. This time, she cringed when she looked at all the money sitting there.

And the money was hers, not another hi-tech scam Bomb had pulled.

Not that she cared.

She would rather sleep on the street than touch that money. Rather starve than use it to buy food.

Yes, it had financed for her time in Asia, where she'd spent the best part of a decade soaking up the deadliest combat systems she could find, but since coming home, she'd barely touched a penny. Now, what she could earn and what she could steal from her targets funded her life.

Life?

Yeah, right.

Well... there was 'the dream'. She'd happily blow the lot on that. *The dream* occasionally gave her a warm glow in moments of dire weakness, but she soon snapped out of such states of self-pity and recognized the situation for what it was. Weakness was a state of mind. If she altered her thinking pattern, she was no longer weak. As for living 'her dream'? By definition, a dream was a fantasy – the money was going nowhere.

Still, in emergencies, it was there to be used. And there was no greater emergency right now than saving the life of the Pool Cleaner's next victim.

She transferred $5,000 from her account to Tad's bank.

Business concluded, he gave her his contact details and an escort home, during which, as a precaution, she accessed her bank the moment she got her phone back and changed the login details to her account.

Despite the welcome outcome, she was uneasy during the return journey. Something gnawed at her.

Time frame? Time frame? There was something about a time frame that didn't fit. But which time frame and who did it involve?

She had to crack this.

Had to.

Tomorrow was three days since the Pool Cleaner had killed.

Tomorrow he'd kill again. If she didn't stop him.

What was it about the time frame?

Something mattered.

Crucially.

But what?

Chapter 24

TESS'S LASER-JET PRINTER spewed out yet another set of documents on the Pool Cleaner job, another set she whipped up and with which she papered the remaining free floor space around her as she sat cross-legged in the middle of her living room floor.

She'd been up most of the night staring at papers. Until she'd fallen asleep in the middle of them. But now it was vital she crack this – a life was at stake. The Pool Cleaner killed on a three-day cycle and this was Day Three. Today, another innocent person would be shot dead.

She gazed at all the papers.

Again.

The same papers.

Again.

The same but in yet another different order.

Again.

Bomb had processed more information which she'd added to the collage in the hope it would help. So far, it hadn't. What was it she couldn't see?

There was a time frame that didn't fit.

A time frame which was just plain wrong.

A time frame which – she hesitated to even think it for fear she'd jinx it – could be the key to the entire Pool Cleaner job. It was here somewhere. She knew it.

She gazed across the white landscape fanned out before her. Branching out from where she sat in the center, rows of information on all the victims, their families, the case, serial killers, and everything else they'd amassed, spread across the floor like the unfurled petals of a gigantic flower, with each petal starting with the most crucial information and ending with the least important.

A time frame was the key.

But which time frame?

What kind of time frame?

Whose time frame?

She picked up the first page of the workup on Della Igomi, the second victim. She scanned it. Replaced it. Picked up the second page. Then picked up the first sheet again.

Della died age thirty-three on March 23 at 3:03 a.m. on East Thirty-Third Street. That was a hell of a lot of threes. And the killings were three days apart. Did that mean anything?

No.

How could it?

That wasn't it. That wasn't what she knew in her gut was wrong. That was pure coincidence. If the Pool Cleaner had a number fetish, he'd have had no idea the perfect target would have presented itself to stake out that club at that time. Della had left Boom Boom when she wanted, not at the whim of her killer. No fire alarm had sounded to conveniently get her outside at that exact time – Tess had checked.

155

She picked up a sheet from Angelique's collection. She'd been shot March 26. Did March 26 have any relevance? She selected particular sheets from those fanned across her floor and cross-referenced them. Was there a birthday or anniversary of anyone in any of the families on that date?

No.

So on March 20 or March 23 – the dates of the other shootings?

No.

Her brow furrowed as she looked at paper after paper after paper.

There was something wrong here. She knew it. She fucking knew it! But what was it?

She scanned the lengths of the three couples' relationships: thirteen months; eight months; thirty-nine months. That meant relationships of February one year to the next year's March; August to the following March; and January through March three years later.

And that meant what exactly?

Nothing.

Absolutely squat. It was just nonsense.

So the times of the shootings? Did they mean anything? 3:03, 9:19, 10:56.

No, of course not. She'd already decided that through considering the time Della had left the club.

So the time frame between the killings? Three days. What was the significance of three days? What could you do in three days that you couldn't do in two or could more than do in four? What did you need exactly three days to achieve?

She closed her eyes and dragged her hands down a face scrunched up with frustration.

She opened her eyes and threw the papers back onto the floor.

"What is it, Fish? What am I missing?"

She gasped.

Froze.

Gazed away into space.

Was it that *she* was missing *something* or was it that *something* was *missing*?

She snatched the handful of papers she'd just cast down. She scanned. Threw away the first, the second, the third. It was here. She'd just seen it. But where?

She slung away the fourth. The fifth. The sixth... She picked the fifth back up.

There.

Angelique's time frame.

She scrambled across the floor. Bits of petal from her meticulously constructed flower scattered beneath her hands and knees.

She grabbed one paper. Glanced over it. Tossed it.

Studied another. Flung it.

A third. Garbage.

Where the hell was it?

She glanced at another. Tossed that too.

Something caught her eye.

She gasped.

Spun.

Pawed away paper after paper until just one remained alone in a clearing. She snatched it up.

She leapt to her feet. Winced and almost fell as her right leg buckled. Her leg dragging, she hobbled over to her backpack. Rummaged inside. Pulled out her notebook. Her hand flashed, flipping page after page after page...

"Where is it? Where the hell is it?"

She was sure it was here.

Sure she remembered correctly.

Where the devil was it?

She gasped again.

Stared at the page of notes.

There!

That was it.

That was the key to the missing piece of the puzzle. She'd stake her life on it.

Chapter 25

LIMPING BACK AND forth over the mess that had once been a beautiful white flower, Tess held her phone to her ear. "Come on. Come on. Come — Joe. Joe, it's Tess Williams." She didn't even wait for him to say anything, she was so eager to get her answers. "The shooting at the church. Angelique's ex – when you said there were no suspicious circumstances, what did you mean?"

Joe, the black detective with the hunched shoulders she'd met at the crime scene, said, "When the deceased is found alone, in a room locked from the inside, with a bottle of sleeping pills and a note our tech guys swear is written in his own handwriting, you don't have to be Einstein to figure out what happened."

She grinned. That was the news she'd been hoping for. That was the key to the whole job. She knew the identity of the Pool Cleaner.

"Joe, that thing Allison won't do – you're gonna get it twice when I see you next."

"Tess, what—"

She hung up.

She waved the paper in her other hand. "Fish, this is it. This is it!"

Tess had been so wrong earlier. So unbelievably wrong. And that was why making generalizations sucked.

Yes, she wore decent but cheap clothes, she was educated, and she loved books. But was she a librarian?

No. That was just a dumb generalization someone might make about her from the limited, superficial facts they had.

She phoned Bomb.

"Yo, Tess."

She couldn't help but blurt everything out. "It's not about racism. The Pool Cleaner doesn't give a shit about race. We've completely fucked up. Cleaning the gene pool is bullshit. Just total bullshit. It's a cover. The killings, the website, everything – it's all just a cover."

"Whoa, slow down there, Tess. You're telling me they weren't racist shootings?"

"No. That's all just a cover."

"You don't think the three dead black women might disagree with you?"

"I'm telling you, it's a cover."

"And the website preaching white supremacy?"

"It's all a cover! Everything's a cover!"

"Okay, okay, I've kind of got that now. But a cover for what?"

"Angelique's ex – Alexander Michael Shaw. He overdosed the day she announced her engagement."

"Now just hang on. You're saying three women are dead because some dude couldn't take getting dumped?"

She spun to pace back across the room again, but her knee gave and she slumped. She caught herself before she fell. "Goddamn it!"

"Sorry, I—"

"No, not you. Listen, it was buried there in all the detail. Maybe if I'd asked for a Level Five on the families your system would've caught it. I don't know. But it doesn't matter – we can still stop him before he kills again."

"Tess, I'm sorry, but I'm just not seeing it."

"Bomb, it's beautiful really. As crimes go, this guy's a genius."

"Then, let's hope the Nobel Prize committee recognizes him and does the right thing."

"Do you want me to hang up and explain it all to Fish?"

"Whoa, whoa, whoa, I'm sorry. I'm listening."

She took a deep breath. "Seven months ago, September 21, Angelique and Christian announced their engagement. That same night, within just a few hours, her ex Alexander Shaw locked himself in his room, wrote a goodbye note to his family, and took an overdose."

"That's it?"

"The father, Brian Shaw, is ex-military."

"Again – *that's it?*"

She huffed. "What more do you want?"

"Some proof would be nice."

"Bomb, I'm telling you, this is our guy."

"Tess, you're saying he blew two innocent women's brains out just so he could shoot a third and pretend it was a racist killing, so no one would look at what his family had gone through and ask questions?"

"Exactly."

"Tess," – he sighed as if exasperated – "that's straight out of Hollywood, sister."

161

"What?" What was he talking about? This was the only explanation that made sense.

Bomb's voice rose as he replied, as if his answer would explain everything to even the dumbest of people. "Jack Reacher?"

"Who's Jack Reacher?"

Again his voice rose the same way. "Tom Cruise?"

"Bomb, you're not helping. Quit fooling around and get your head in the game. It's all a cover, I tell you. A goddamn cover."

Brian Shaw, aka the Pool Cleaner, wasn't a racist. He didn't shoot black women because he was racist. This wasn't about race in the least. This was personal. Deeply, deeply personal. This was about one woman. A woman he held responsible for destroying his family. Everything and everybody who got in the way was merely collateral damage.

She could almost see Bomb shaking his head. She heard him cluck his tongue. But she was right. She had to be.

Finally, he said, "I don't know. That's a big ask."

"He's got the motive; he's got the training."

"We don't have his military record. Who's to say he wasn't just a cook?"

Tess liked the way Bomb saw the other side of things. Liked the way he wasn't afraid to challenge her. Liked the way he could see things she couldn't. But he was wrong on this.

"Hack his record. Now. I'll give you one hundred to one he can strip an M4 in under sixty seconds but hasn't a clue what to do with oregano."

"Okay. Give me ten and I'll get back to you."

Ten minutes? How the devil did he expect her to sit on her hands for ten whole minutes after a revelation like this one? Unfortunately, she knew she had no choice – the Pool Cleaner would kill again today, so if she got this wrong, not only wouldn't she nail him, but another innocent victim would die. And just because Bomb had said ten minutes didn't actually mean it would be ten. Not at the speed he worked. No, it could be eight, five, maybe even three.

She hung up. But then simply sat staring at her phone, praying for it to ring.

Chapter 26

CLUTCHING HER PHONE, Tess lurched across her living room again, her mind in hyperdrive. Parents should never have to bury their children. It was so wrong. On so many levels. And if such a parent blamed another person for their loss, a demand for justice could see blind fury unleashed upon anyone who stood in their way.

Angelique's ex, Alexander Michael Shaw, had taken his own life because of the loss he felt.

His father, Brian Shaw, had taken other people's lives because of the loss inflicted upon him.

Brian Shaw shot black women, but was he a racist?

The Pool Cleaner might be a racist; he might not be. But there was one thing about which Tess had absolutely no doubt – this job revolved around white supremacy as much as her life revolved around the Dewey decimal system.

He was a wounded father. A father who wanted payback. A father with a military background. A father with a viciously ingenious plan. A plan that he couldn't abandon now because too many questions would be raised.

The Pool Cleaner would have to strike again. He'd have to cover his tracks. He'd have to amass so many truly random victims no one would ever stop to ask questions about his one prime target – a target hidden in plain sight.

Yes, the Pool Cleaner would kill again. Today. If Tess couldn't reach him in time.

She grabbed her backpack and slung various items inside. As injured as she was, she needed all the protection she could get to go up against ex-military. She pulled on elasticized elbow and knee protectors, struggling to get the last one over her heavily strapped right knee.

Next, she velcroed each of her bespoke seven-inch-long titanium alloy forearm guards in place, followed by her shin guards. Ergonomically contoured and less than one inch wide, the three-sided guards hugged her limbs perfectly and enabled her to defend against weapons and, when used offensively, to break bones.

She glanced at the time: 12:47 p.m. The Pool Cleaner had already shot both Angelique and Della by this time of the day. He could be lining up his next victim in his rifle scope that very second. Squeezing the trigger that very second. Ending another innocent life – "Come on, Bomb." She glared at her phone.

Whipping off her shirt, she hobbled for her closet. She snatched her Stealth body armor. Threat Level IIIA, the streamlined bulletproof vest could stop a .44 Magnum. Unfortunately, the Pool Cleaner didn't use a Magnum, but a rifle with far more power. She'd have to pray she could get close enough to kill him before he got a shot off at her. Velcroing the vest in place, she limped back to her backpack.

Her leg was stronger and more stable today after a day's rest and treatment, but it wasn't good. That could be a problem. Her ribs? She didn't even want to think about her ribs. If it came to it, she'd have to pray adrenaline would allow her to fight through the pain. She looked at her pocket-sized medical kit as she popped it into her pack.

Medication would normally have been an option. But against ex-Special Forces? In her condition, she'd need to be as sharp as possible, not as high as a junkie who'd found a prescription pad.

No, she'd have to rely on her bandaging and posthypnotic suggestions.

She huffed.

The strapping helped for moving around her apartment, but for one-on-one combat with a trained killer? Hell, was she in trouble.

"Come on, Bomb."

She pulled a lightweight leather jacket from a hanger and slung it on. Checked the mirror. Together with her shirt, it fully concealed her vest to all but the most practiced of eyes. Plus, it being leather, it offered a further layer of protection.

Grabbing her armored gloves from her drawer, she glanced at her ringing phone on the bed. She snatched it. "Well?"

Bomb said, "As usual, you were right – ex-Special Forces. Served in Iraq. Afghanistan. Even got a Bronze Star. Honorably discharged on medical grounds after he lost a finger in a firefight in Kandahar. Was later diagnosed with PTSD."

"I knew it."

"There's something else – he's got a monthly subscription to TunnelGhost.com, a VPN provider."

VPN meant he could use the Web with complete anonymity, for example, to update GodsPoolCleaner.com.

"It's him, Bomb. I'm telling you, it's him."

"Tess, this only confirms he *could* be our guy, not that he *is*. Okay, he fits your scenario, but we've got absolutely squat that places him at any of the scenes with a gun in his hand."

She pushed the button for Fish's automatic feeding machine to start – that would keep him going for a week if she was... detained.

She said, "Bomb, it's Day Three. If he is our boy, we don't need evidence because he'll be stalking a new victim – we can catch him with his finger on the trigger."

Bomb said, "Get me a cell phone number and I'll get you a location."

She yanked open her apartment door. "Already on it."

She slammed the door shut behind her.

The clock was ticking.

Did she have hours? Minutes? Or was she already too late?

167

Chapter 27

"**HE WAS WITHDRAWN** when he got back from Afghanistan," said Susan Shaw. Sitting on her cream sofa, she stroked a white cat sitting in her lap. "He seemed to have difficulty connecting with people, even with me and Alex."

Tess said, "It must've been very hard for you."

"It was. Remembering how good things used to be."

Susan sighed and looked at a gold framed photo on the wall of a smiling family hugging each other – husband Brian, herself, and in the middle, their toddler son Alexander. Her curly brown hair wasn't streaked with gray in the photo.

As for Brian?

Tess glanced to another photo on the mantel of him in uniform – a big, mean mountain of square-jawed brutality. Now heading for fifty, he was getting on for twice Tess's age, but with nearly two decades of military experience, he was deadly. And that was without factoring in her ribs and knee problems.

Susan said, "He'd never talk about what happened over there. But it must've been bad. He was always such a strong man. Strongest man I've ever known. I mean, you don't get to be Special Forces by being soft, do you, so what happened over there, heaven only knows."

"But in all the years since his discharge, hasn't there been any improvement?" said Tess. She'd been in such a rush to get out and confirm Brian Shaw as the Pool Cleaner, she'd had to concoct a cover story en route. Luckily, she still had all Meg Richards's information in her bag so she'd opted for an insurance claim story.

"Oh, things slowly got better, yes. And were really quite good for a good long while. But why's all this suddenly important again, Miss Richards?"

Tess smiled. "It's just a formality, so don't worry, but if our company is to issue a disability payment to your husband, we need to know how your family situation has worsened recently."

"I didn't even know he'd made a claim."

"He may not have. It's quite normal for military personnel discharged on medical grounds to come under review from time to time. We like to take care of those who take care of us." Tess smiled again.

"Well, with Alex doing so well in college and with Brian getting a new job, things seemed to be turning around – it really looked like we were going to be a real family again. But then that girl came along, didn't she?"

"That girl?" Tess leaned forward in the cream-colored armchair.

"Angelique Marley."

Even though she didn't need them, Tess scribbled notes in her notebook to look convincing.

Susan said, "That conniving little tramp got poor Alex all turned about. He was a straight A student till he

169

met her – never drank, never partied, never took money from my pocketbook without asking."

"She was a bad influence?"

"That girl would test the Lord Jesus himself, so she would. We tried to warn Alex that she was trouble and only saw him as a meal ticket, but… Well, you can't tell young love, can you?"

Tess shook her head to empathize. "You certainly can't."

"She was spending all his money. Nagging him to take her out all the time. He was nowhere near graduating, but she was pushing him to apply for jobs he didn't want just because they were well paid."

"And this put stress on your family?"

"Brian tried to talk some sense into Alex, but I could see what was happening – that woman had him so twisted about, if we'd pushed too hard, we'd have lost him."

Tess said, "So you put up with her to keep the family together."

Susan's eyes filled with tears. "And then she met that Hawthorne boy and, my, the money that family has. So…" Her chin trembled. She pulled out a tissue and sniffled into it, obviously struggling not to cry in front of a stranger.

"And Alex couldn't get over that?"

"He begged her to come back. Begged her. But… He flunked his exams. Locked himself in his room for days on end. Doctor Phillips put him on medication. We begged him to see a therapist. To talk things through, you know. But he just wouldn't listen. He was so sure she'd come back to him. Then, September 21…"

170

Susan Shaw sobbed. Tess put her hand on her knee. "I'm sorry to bring up such painful memories, Mrs. Shaw. I've lost someone close to me, so I know how it hurts."

"I still think I see him on the street sometimes. But when I look it's someone else. Last night, by mistake, I made three cups of coffee instead of two."

"And how did what happened affect Brian?"

"Brian? Brian just wasn't Brian anymore. Still isn't. I just don't recognize him. It's like I lost two people that day. Lost my whole family. And all because of that money-grabbing little... little slut."

"So Brian still isn't right?"

"It's just not him anymore. It's like he just shut down. We don't talk; we don't go out; we don't... We just don't have a life." She dabbed her tears away. "He blames me, you see. Blames me for persuading him to accept that girl. Sometimes, I wish he'd just hit me and then maybe we could move on."

She wept.

Tess didn't know what to say, so just gave her a little time and squeezed her hand – human contact could mean so much to those starved of affection.

Susan waved her hand in the air. "I don't care what Father Patrick might think and if I have to burn in Hell for saying it, but I'm not sorry about what happened to that girl. She was wicked. Wicked through and through. Some people just are."

Tess knew the pain of loss. Though she hated religion, hated the way it controlled people and spread misinformation, she knew it could bring solace to some. She squeezed Susan's hand. "I'm sure Father Patrick would understand. After all, why would we ever need Hell if there were no bad people?"

Susan gave Tess half a smile. "Thank you, Miss Richards."

"Would it be possible to have a word with Mr. Shaw, please?"

"If you can find him. I never know where the heck he is nowadays."

"He's out a lot?"

Susan nodded. "Uh-huh."

"Was he out Saturday morning?"

"As far as I remember."

"How about last Wednesday night?"

"Wednesday?" She thought for a moment. "Wednesday he was working all night. He'd pulled another double shift – not that you'd know it from what he brings home."

"A week ago Sunday? Was he working then too?"

She thought for a moment. "Ah, yes, he was. Most of the day. He finally trailed in around ten. Barely said a word."

The Pool Cleaner's first victim had been shot at 9:09.

Brian Shaw was the Pool Cleaner. Tess would take a thousand-to-one odds-on bet with anyone on that.

"Do you have a cell phone number I can reach him on, please?"

172

Chapter 28

WITH WHAT LOOKED like crumbs from a Danish caught in his moustache, the cab driver looked back at Tess in his rear seat. "Lady, this is still costing you even though we ain't going nowhere."

Tess stared at her phone, yet again willing it to ring. "That's okay." She glanced out of the window of the stationary cab at La Nouvelle. To herald the arrival of the new season's fashions, a blue dress with yellow flowers hung center stage in the window. Hideous.

She needed to leave here. She'd only traveled five hundred yards from the Shaws' so she wouldn't be seen and cause suspicion, but she couldn't go any further because she had no idea which was the correct direction – while one would be the right one and take her closer to the killer, the other three would all take her further away. Further away from the innocent black woman who the Pool Cleaner was going to slaughter just to solidify his public persona.

Staring at her phone, she prayed it would ring, that she wouldn't arrive just in time to hear a rifle shot, see blood spatter the sidewalk, watch a life fall apart.

Her phone didn't ring.

With her body armor on, her clothes on top, and her injuries nagging at her, sweat trickled from Tess's brow. She yanked at her jacket collar to waft cool air inside. Unfortunately, she couldn't risk taking it off for her sweaty, clinging shirt to reveal the outline of her bullet-proof vest – what better way to arouse suspicion?

Her phone rang. "Bomb?"

"Six forty-five Hillington Avenue."

She leapt forward in her seat. "Six twenty Hillington Avenue. How long?"

The driver shrugged. "Er… thirty-five minutes."

"There's an extra 300 if you make it twenty."

"I'll do what I can, but I ain't promising, lady."

The cab jerked away from the curb.

Bomb said, "Three stories. First floor: laundromat. Floors two and three: apartments, all occupied."

"So, he's on the roof."

"That's my guess."

"Thanks, Bomb." She almost hung up.

"Tess, you're all busted up and he's Special Forces. We could call 911. "

An anonymous tip might see the police respond. It might not. But she was sure they wouldn't respond before the Pool Cleaner's website updated with news of a fresh kill. And even if they did respond, and even if they did catch him in time, what would happen? Would he get the chair? Not in New York State, he wouldn't. No, he'd get a nice warm room and three squares a day, and the possibility of one day getting parole after being 'cured' of his temporary insanity.

"He's mine." She hung up.

She prayed that part of Hillington Avenue was just normal buildings and there wasn't a park or anything substantial in between 620 and 645 making it a significant distance between the two. She couldn't risk being identified as having been dropped at 645.

She gazed out at the buildings flying by. She'd made the most obvious generalization she could to track down the Pool Cleaner. A generalization that no one would have imagined could ever be wrong given the 'evidence' available. And, as with most generalizations, it had been wildly inaccurate because it missed all the hidden layers that made people such complex characters.

If she hadn't jumped to the most obvious conclusion – that he was the racist his choice of victim and website decreed he was – she might have caught him days ago and he wouldn't be out hunting another innocent victim now. She had to finish this. She had to finish it and be sure it was finished.

Tess now knowing his backstory, she might have sympathized and let him get away with it, if he'd only killed the scheming slut Angelique. But his elaborate plan had meant innocents had to die to see him not just evade capture, but evade suspicion. For that, he had to pay. And she'd take that payment in blood.

But the clock was ticking.

Ticking faster and faster and faster.

She leaned forward as her taxi sped past an SUV. "Can we go any faster?"

"Lady, you want a cab to Hillington, or a hearse to the morgue?"

Every second counted. Literally. If a white man and a black woman strolled along Hillington Avenue, blood would spatter the sidewalk. Could she get there in time to stop the Pool Cleaner and save the next victim?

Chapter 29

HOBBLING UP THE steps as fast as she could in 645 Hillington Avenue's gloomy emergency exit stairwell, Tess dragged on her armored gloves. She was one hundred percent sure she'd find the Pool Cleaner here. Everything pointed at Brian Shaw. Everything.

No matter how expert a killer was, they always made at least one mistake. No one was perfect.

So what was the Pool Cleaner's mistake?

The Pool Cleaner could have killed Angelique any day over the past eight months and gotten away with it. Any day. But he chose her wedding day. He chose to make a statement. He chose to revel in his revenge. If he'd looked at it as simply killing someone, he'd have walked free. But he made it personal. He made it about punishing someone. Had he not, Tess would probably never have questioned whether it was a random killing or not, and he could've walked away from his alter ego's killing spree to live a long and happy life.

Yes, if there was one thing she'd learned in all her years it was to never overlook the stupidity of people.

As she grabbed the metal banister rail to fly around the small concrete landing midway between floors two and three, her right knee gave. She crashed onto cold gray steps.

"Goddamn it." She scrambled to her feet, wincing as she put weight on her right leg. If her knee gave out once she was on the roof, she might never make it down to ground level again – unless it was in a body bag, or after being thrown off the roof by the Pool Cleaner himself.

But she couldn't think like that. Doubt clouded the mind. Invited misjudgment. Forced errors. She needed focus. She needed to block the pain and visualize the fight to come – and her winning it.

She forced herself on. Hobbling as quickly as she could. Pushing pain from her reality.

She had to reach the top. The clock was ticking down the seconds to the Pool Cleaner claiming his next victim.

Every second mattered.

At least, the lack of police cruiser sirens outside the building meant he hadn't yet struck.

But that could change literally any second.

While racing up the last flight of stairs, she slowed her breathing. She would normally have drawn in for four seconds, held it for four, and exhaled for four, but the extra effort needed to control her pain and sharpen her focus wouldn't allow her full breathing technique. Pounding up the steps, she panted like a couch potato forced to run for a bus.

She had to do something.

She needed to slow her breathing to slow her body's fight-or-flight response. Adrenaline could dull pain and sharpen reflexes, but only in the right doses. Uncontrolled, too much flooding her body could cause a

177

freeze response, or tunnel vision, or impeded thinking, any of which would make her vulnerable, and with her injuries, she was already vulnerable enough.

Unable to count her breathing, she pushed her mind to focus on the mechanics of the confrontation to come, instead of on the danger and impending injury. Eliminating as much of the emotional element as she could would help control her body's responses.

Reaching the door to the roof at the top of the stairs, she didn't have time to compose herself. Not even to knead her earlobe to massage away the pain. Any second that shot could ring out. She had to stop him.

She slung her backpack into the darkest corner and after taking just one deep breath to steady her weary limbs, she slowly levered down the emergency handle on the door. Despite her care, it clunked as it opened. She prayed the noise from the street would've drowned it out to anyone on the roof.

She eased the door open.

A shaft of sunlight shot into the stairwell.

She peeked out.

A flat gravel roof. More roofs stretching out across the street. Beyond – a smudged gray sky and the city skyline.

No killer.

The doorway faced across the roof, parallel to the road. That left one corner overlooking the street that she couldn't see.

Stepping into the light, she winced. But not with pain – the tar and gravel roof crunched under her feet. Most of the gravel wasn't loose, but wear and the elements had loosened enough. How could she hope to creep up on someone?

178

Her back sliding along the stairwell block's wall, she moved around to see the corner hidden from her. She ducked under a metal bar sticking out of the wall at shoulder height. In a third-rate movie, the villain would get impaled on that. If only real life were so simple.

At the edge of the wall, she stopped. She took one last breath and then poked her head out as quickly as she could and then pulled it straight back in.

The Pool Cleaner!

Chapter 30

TESS PEEKED AROUND the wall again. On the edge of the roof, aiming a rifle at the sidewalk across the street, a man crouched within the metal struts supporting a billboard advertising cola. Because he was in the shadows and mostly obscured by the billboard, anyone looking up wouldn't see him, while his rifle's barrel would merely appear to be part of the billboard's tubular metal support framework.

Tess prayed his cleverness in choosing his position would prove his biggest mistake – not only would it hide him from the street, it would hide her from him if she approached directly from behind. She shuffled over into position.

Next to a cluster of raised air vents lay a bag of golf clubs – a club being around the same length as a rifle, that must be how he carried his weapon around the city without being stopped.

The seconds were ticking away. Any moment that trigger could see blood and brain splattering the sidewalk. She needed to stop him. Fast.

He stood forty-five feet away. She could either sprint over and hope she got to him before he heard her and turned with his gun, or she could creep over and hope he was so focused on his task he'd never notice until it was too late. Yes, she had her vest on, but that was only good for handguns – there was no way it would stop a rifle shot at close range.

Fearing she'd make too much noise running, especially with her leg injury, she crept forward. The gravel ground under her feet. The traffic below drowned out the sound to all but her. But the closer she got to her target, the more likely her noisy approach would give her away.

Closer and closer she edged. Ready to leap into action in a split second.

Now only thirty-five feet.

The Pool Cleaner stayed fixed on his objective.

Closer.

Twenty-five feet.

Still no sign he was aware of her presence.

Closer.

Twenty feet.

Still no movement.

Closer.

Fifteen feet.

She had him. It took the average person 1.5 seconds to respond to an unexpected stimulus. The Pool Cleaner would be no different. Just a couple more steps and he'd never be able to react in time even if he heard her.

Down on the street, a car alarm wailed. That would disturb the Pool Cleaner's focus. Once disturbed, his mind would be free to focus on other sights, smells… sounds.

Tess froze. Cringed.

Her left foot raised in mid-stride, she was too worried to place it on the roof for fear of the noise it might make. Her whole body tensed.

She waited. Held her breath. Sweat beaded on her brow. Her injured right knee trembled under the strain.

But the Pool Cleaner didn't react.

After what felt like five minutes even though it was likely no more than five seconds, she put her foot down and took a gulp of air.

Just another step and she'd be close enough.

But the Pool Cleaner turned for a bottle of water near his feet.

He saw her.

Froze. For what felt like an age but in reality was only around 1.5 seconds.

Maneuvering his rifle out from amidst the metal framework, he twisted around as he stood to shoot.

But if you were already primed to strike, 1.5 seconds was an eternity in which to act. Tess was primed – she pounced.

Before he had time to aim and shoot, Tess grabbed the rifle barrel with one hand, keeping it pointing past her body, while her other palm heeled him in the nose.

He recoiled, blood splattering across his face.

Both her hands on the weapon and his grip loosened by pain, she twisted the rifle and yanked it up.

She slammed the barrel into his face.

Once.

Twice.

Three times.

He staggered back, dazed and bloody.

An opening made, she tossed the rifle away across the roof. A woman killing a man in unarmed combat could easily argue self-defense in court. A woman shooting an unarmed man? Unless she was very lucky, that woman was pretty much screwed.

She thrust a knee strike into him. A move that had worked fine in her mirror. In her mirror in her safe, warm apartment, where her target was not moving and not trying to hit her back. Here on the roof…?

Her right leg buckled and she staggered, trying to catch her balance.

A fist rocketed for her head.

She threw her arms up to block a flurry of punches.

He smashed a hand into her titanium alloy guards. If not for the adrenaline pumping through his body, his broken knuckles would have been unbearably painful. An ordinary fight would have been all but over now.

Unfortunately for Tess, Special Forces personnel were trained to fight through pain. He recoiled, but then came all the stronger.

His momentary hesitation was all Tess needed. Having had that split second to regroup, she swung a right cross, then a left hook, then poked out a knee-level kick. But hampered by her injuries, her moves were sluggish.

With relative ease, he parried the punches and then leapt back from the kick.

As if a mountain of square-jawed brutality wasn't mean enough, he whipped out a hunting knife.

He slashed at her.

She let it glance safely off the side of her titanium forearm guard.

She counterattacked, slamming a roundhouse kick into the side of his thigh to deaden the leg.

He staggered back.

But twisting into her kick ripped pain through her midriff. She cried out and hunched over.

He saw her weakness. Pounced.

She dodged his next slashing blade.

With her knee both injured and heavily strapped, she didn't have the split-second mobility that made her a supreme fighter – she didn't see the punch from his other hand until too late, so she couldn't get out of the way in time.

Flinging an arm up in the vain hope of blocking the strike, she tried to twist to ride with the blow.

Again, her rib injury stole her fluidity.

While her turning movement sapped it of much of its power, the fist hit her in the side of the head. Spun her around.

With her back exposed and unprotected, the Pool Cleaner struck.

The knife raked down Tess's back.

She gasped. Arched her back. Twisted away.

Thank God for her body armor.

Sidestepping, she spun around to face him anew. Lacking her usual strength and mobility, she couldn't risk taking on a skilled knife-fighter a moment longer. She had to neutralize that threat.

As he slashed again, she sprang closer to shut his knife hand down. She hacked her hands into his arm, not just stopping the blade from hitting her, but attacking the muscle.

The shock to his tissue forced his grip to loosen and the knife flew from his grasp.

She slammed a hammerfist into the side of his head. A crunching elbow followed.

Her thumb tucked in to let her hit with the hard bone at the base of her index finger, her ridge hand strike crashed into his groin.

She grabbed him. Twisted. Heaved him over her hip and hurled him on the ground.

But the pain in her ribs kicked like a horse.

Arghh! She fell to her knees.

From the ground, he grabbed her. Slammed her down on the gravel.

Wrapping his legs over her torso, left across her neck, right over her chest, he locked her right arm over his body, immobilizing her.

He heaved back, straining her arm against its joints.

With his leg across her throat, she couldn't breathe. She had to escape or it was game over.

She heaved to maneuver and break his hold the way she normally would. Pain again ripped through her body, stopping her from moving how she needed to.

She was caught fast.

Her mind flew through all the grappling escapes she'd learned over the years. All the Krav Maga techniques Harry had taught her in his Brooklyn basement. All the times Ayumi had pinned her in the dojo in Okayama and tormented her till she fathomed the release. All the pain, all the bruises, all the torture. She remembered it all. Everything. It was ingrained into her. Ingrained so that in a deadly situation, she'd always be able to fight her way out.

She twisted.

Jerked.

Clawed.

Wriggled.

Bucked.

Tried everything her panicked mind could recall.

Nothing worked.

With all her injuries, she couldn't gain the positions or the leverage the moves demanded.

He was too strong.

His hold too tight.

There was no escape.

She felt the last of her strength draining from her body, just as the last of her thoughts felt like it was wading through thick mud. She couldn't breathe. This was the end.

The martial arts were renowned for gravity-defying acrobatics, bone-shattering power, and secret death strikes. But sometimes, the simplest move was the best move...

With the last of her strength, she managed to twist clamp her jaws to his calf. She bit.

He yanked back on her arm, obviously hoping to fight through the pain long enough to kill her.

But she ground her teeth. Shook her head like a rabid beast.

He screamed. Let go.

She rolled away. Gasped for air. Felt life surging back into her body with every breath.

But she didn't have time to spend recovering.

She clambered to her feet.

Looked for him.

His leg hurt from her bite, he hobbled away across the roof.

For escape?

No.

For his gun.

She had to reach him before he reached it.

She raced after him, her right leg dragging. She repeated to herself, 'Pain is a breath I blow out'. Every gasp of air saw her stronger as the pain left her body.

He was almost at the gun.

But she was almost on him.

She leapt to fly past him. Feet first.

In midair, she grabbed his head. Locked it under her right arm.

She slammed into the gravel, dragging him, face-first. As she hit, she wrenched his head backwards.

His neck vertebrae crunched.

His body twitched. Then lay motionless. Silent. Breathless.

Tess lay there, panting. Her mind a flood of blood and gore and carnage.

She closed her eyes.

She pictured a tall snow-capped mountain. A towering forest. Blue sky. A reflection in a tranquil lake. Total serenity.

Her breathing slowed.

When she finally rolled away from the body to get up, she cried out. Gingerly, she struggled to her feet. The fight over, her adrenaline exhausted, her razor sharp focus relaxing, her body was free to feel every scrap of pain coursing through it. She limped over to the roof door, clutching her side and gasping with every breath.

The bag of golf clubs caught her eye. When a single club could fetch a couple of hundred dollars brand new, a decent set would cover all her rents for at least a week. Even after she'd paid for shipping to her fence.

She checked the clubs weren't personalized, then slung the bag over her shoulder. An added bonus was that not only would they help fund her work, but when she was back down on the street, the bag would hide the knife slash in the back of her jacket.

She yanked the door open, but looked back at the body of the Pool Cleaner. Susan Shaw had lost her husband years ago. Would she mourn him now? Probably. But then she'd move on and live a better life than she ever could have otherwise. Tess hadn't ended Susan Shaw's life – she'd given her a new one. Or at least that's what Tess was going to believe.

She limped into the stairwell.

The door slammed shut.

Chapter 31

WITH HIS BASEBALL cap on backwards, the boy pressed his head against the window of Nico's Ices, staring at the stainless steel trays of ice creams – a multicolored patchwork quilt of deliciousness.

"Which one, honey?" said the woman with a figure so trim it was doubtful she'd ever even looked at ice cream before, let alone passed it between her lips.

He pointed. "Strawberry." Turning, he grinned up at her, eyes sparkling with delight.

All around, pedestrians bustled down the street, shopping for this, indulging in that.

In their midst, like a black wave churning up a tranquil ocean, a scrawny black guy slunk along. Head down studying his phone, he didn't care whose shoulder he bumped; he didn't care who had to step out of his way; he didn't care that other people had lives to lead too. He was obviously way too important to be bothered about other people's tiny struggles with their tiny lives.

He took a swig from a cup with big bamboo style letters on the side saying 'Coffee Shack'.

Suddenly, a shadow reared before him. He didn't look up. Just stopped and waited for it to realize it had to move.

It didn't move.

Instead, it knocked his phone out of his hand.

He glared at the obstacle. "Motherfuck—" He realized who it was.

Tess said, "Do you want to pick that up?"

His gaze crawled across her face, across the fat lip he and his friends had given her, across the bruising and gash on her forehead that they'd inflicted. But his friends weren't here today.

Scrawny Guy didn't say a word, but locked her gaze as he slowly sank to the ground to retrieve his phone.

Just as his fingers were about to touch it, Tess kicked his hand.

He yelped and whipped his hand back. The coffee in his other hand splattered all over the sidewalk.

Under her foot, Tess slid the phone to her right and then stepped nearer to an alleyway, leaving the phone between them once more.

She smiled. "Do you want to pick that up?"

He scowled at her. But then crept forward and bent down again.

And again she smashed her foot into his reaching hand.

He ripped his hand away. "Motherfucking whore."

She slapped him across the face. "Language!"

He glared, hatred drilling into her.

Again, she clawed the phone further toward the alley under her shoe.

190

His nostrils flared. His breathing snorted. Fury burned in his eyes.

She wanted him to hit her, to kick her, to head-butt her. To do anything that would give her legitimate reason to stamp this insect into the ground. But more, she wanted to break him. Show him how inconsequential he truly was and how she – *a mere woman* – could destroy his entire world in a blink. The city would be a safer, nicer place with one less egotistical, chauvinistic asshole strolling through it.

He looked at his phone, then back up at her.

She smiled. "Now, what's that magic word again?"

His top lip curled into a sneer. It trembled. But he said, "Please can I pick up my phone?"

He was either going to apologize and back down. Let a small woman better him. Or he was going to bleed. The choice was his. But that didn't mean she couldn't help him make up his mind.

She kicked out. The phone skittered right between his feet, off the sidewalk, and into the street. A truck ran over it.

She put her hand to her mouth. "Oops."

His breathing rasped. His gaze jumped frenziedly from one thing to another. His fists clenched and unclenched.

She'd chosen her spot purposefully: no traffic cameras overlooking it; a wide sidewalk so people could pass without getting involved; a deserted alleyway to her right in which to conclude business. But she couldn't attack him cold – he had to attack her so she could justify the payback she was going to demand.

She stared at him. Oh, God, how he ached to hit her.

"Do it, you pussy," said Tess. "Come on, I dare you."

He lunged at her.

She sidestepped.

Caught one of his arms.

Whipped him around and slammed him face-first into the side of a dumpster in the alley.

She pulled back her fist to slam it into one of his kidneys—

Someone caught her hand. Held it fast.

Oh shit, was it one of his friends who she hadn't seen?

She spun to attack, but gasped.

Froze.

Oh, God, not now. Please, not now.

A police badge hung in the air before her.

"Whoa, easy there, tiger." A man smiled at her. A man she knew. "What's the problem here?"

Scrawny Guy turned, blood trickling from his nose. "This bitch done busted up my phone is what the problem is here."

Detective Josh 'Pompous Dick' Hardy looked up at the size of the tall black guy and then down at the size of Tess. Then he looked at her bruised face.

He said, "I don't see any phone, but I do see a woman covered in bruises being threatened by an aggressive asshole. Now, do I need to paint you a picture of what's going to happen in exactly three seconds, or do you want to take off while I'm feeling generous?"

"But she—"

Josh counted. "One... Two..."

Scrawny Guy scurried away. Almost around the corner of the alley, he turned back. "I'll see you again, bitch. You see if I don't." He ducked out of sight.

The detective winced looking at her facial injuries. "Are you okay?"

"Oh, this? It's nothing. I take a self-defense class. You get the odd bruise."

"The odd bruise? Hey, I don't want to upset you, but some folk just aren't cut out for combat, you know. You ever thought of taking up a less dangerous hobby?"

She huffed. "Like flower arranging?"

He held his hands up defensively. "Hey, I'm only saying. Look, you got lucky today and pulled off one of those crappy moves they teach in those lame classes. But what do you think would've happened if I hadn't come along, huh? Did you see the size of that guy?"

Like a Shakespearean actor being heckled on stage, she had no choice but to bite her tongue and stay in character.

She sighed. "You're right. Sorry. I guess I just got carried away in the moment." She smiled up at him, her hero. "Thanks for your help. See you 'round."

She turned to go.

"Hey, whoa there, tiger!" He caught her arm.

Tess turned back. He'd played the hero; now what the hell did he want?

Josh said, "That guy might still be hanging around. Do you think I'm just going to let you waltz straight back into trouble?"

She had to get rid of him. "Don't sweat it. It's only like a stone's throw to my place." It wasn't, but he didn't know that.

"Listen, you won't believe what can happen in just a few seconds. Trust me, you're not safe with an asshole like that around." He gently placed his hand in the small of her back. "Come on, I'll walk you home."

No way could she let anyone know where she lived. Especially a cop.

She said, "But I've got some errands to run."

"No problem." He pointed left out of the alley. "There's a little coffee shop just around the corner. I'll buy you a drink and I promise you, by the time you've drunk it, he'll have gotten bored and have found some other poor schlep to victimize, so you can get on with your day. Okay?"

"But—"

"Hey, do I look like the kind of guy who takes no for an answer?" He smiled at her.

Oh, goddamnit. Staying in character really sucked. Not only could she not kick Scrawny Guy's ass, but now she had to go for coffee with the handsome hero who'd rescued her from the wicked villain. Had to.

Could the day get any worse?

"That's, er…" Oh, hell, what could she possibly say to get out of this? Was there anything? She couldn't risk offending him in case they ever met again and she needed something from him.

Smiling a roguish smile, he raised his eyebrows.

She smiled back. "That's very kind. Thank you. But you have to let me buy. It's the least I can do."

They meandered out of the alley and turned left toward Marlowe's Grounds.

She glanced at the rugged detective. If in uniform in a bar, he could easily be mistaken for a male stripper. He seemed pleasant enough too. Far more amenable than the pompous dick she'd met in Riverside Park. But there was something off about this guy. She didn't know what. Something just gave her a bad feeling.

Usually, she didn't mind courting the friendship of cops because they came in so useful for her work, but this guy? Should she risk it?

No. She'd smile at his conversation, down her coffee quickly, and be out of there in ten minutes – long enough to be polite, but not so long that he got too comfortable.

Josh said, "So, which martial art are you studying?"

"It's kind of like MMA."

"Oh, yeah?" He grinned. "Fancy yourself as a little Bruce Lee, huh?"

The grandfather of modern martial arts, Bruce Lee had brought Kung Fu out of the secret shadows of the East and into the West for all to share and marvel at. Ironically, he'd died young and never known the legacy he'd left. She'd die happy if she could have just one percent of the impact on the world he'd had.

She said, "Well, you can't always rely on a guy being around to protect you, can you?"

He snickered. "Seriously, you have to be careful with that self-defense crap. I've seen it so many times, you won't believe – some woman takes a few classes, practices kicking a guy in the nuts a few times and sees him dutifully fall down, and suddenly she thinks she's goddamn invincible. I tell you, you try that crap on the street, it won't only be a busted lip you get."

"So a woman just has to resign herself to being a victim?"

"No, of course not. But you've got to learn the right stuff and then you've got to really drill it so it comes without having to think about it."

"Yeah?"

He nodded. "I could give you a few tips, if you like. Maybe stop you getting your ass kicked so much."

She smiled. A big beaming smile. "That would be great. Thanks." Today just kept getting better and better.

Yep, staying in character sucked ass.

What the hell would go wrong next?

The End.
Continue the adventure with *Blood Justice* (book #3).
Grab it now: **http://stevenleebooks.com/jpwb**
Or flip the page for a sneak peek.

Blood Justice

Angel of Darkness Book 03

Blood Justice Extract

"**DON'T GO OUT** there, please." Cloaked in darkness in their bedroom doorway, Jessica clung to his bare arm so tightly that her fingernails dug into his flesh.

Like he wanted to go outside in the middle of the night, not knowing what was lurking out there, waiting for him. But something had made those strange metallic clunking and creaking sounds to wake them, so did he have a choice?

Standing in just his white shorts, he peered through the gloom engulfing the staircase and down to their front door. He tried to swallow, but his mouth was so dry that it was as if the muscles in his throat had seized.

He rubbed a hand over his face and gulped air, his heart pounding like he'd just done an extra half hour on the treadmill at BodyWise. His hand trembled, so he tensed the muscles to stop it, hoping Jessica wouldn't see how scared he was. But no matter how hard he fought it, he couldn't stop the shaking.

Jessica's big brown eyes gazed up at him like those of a puppy pleading to be held. "Please, David. You don't know who's out there."

Cupping his cheek, she turned him to look at her square on.

She spoke so quietly, it was barely a whisper. "Please."

Fear lined and twisted her features, yet she was still the most beautiful woman he'd ever seen. High cheekbones, full lips, porcelain skin. Like someone off the cover of a magazine.

He gripped the decorative Samurai sword they'd bought last fall at that flea market in Williamsburg. It wasn't razor sharp like a real one, but he'd sliced a melon clean in two in the yard with it, so it felt mighty reassuring. "What if they take my new truck? Or my tools? How are we gonna make the mortgage if I can't work?"

"You'll get new ones. The insurance will cover it."

He blew out a heavy breath and turned away, rubbing his hand over this mouth. "You know, er..."

"You said you'd renewed the policy."

"Yeah, well, you asked me in front of your dad and like I was gonna let him know we're struggling."

Another metallic creak came from outside. Something big was being prized apart. In unison, their heads turned toward the door.

Someone was trying to get into his garage. It had to be. And he couldn't let them. If he lost either his truck or his tools, he wouldn't be able to work. No way could they survive on Jessica's paycheck alone. They'd lose everything. Not just the truck and the tools, but the house – everything.

Like hell was that going to happen. If some asshole thought they were going to mess with his truck, his tools, his life, hell, were they in for one shitload of pain.

Tightening his grip on the sword, he pulled away from Jessica and lunged for the stairs.

But she grabbed his arm again, anchoring him there. "Wait for the police. Please." Tears sparkled in her eyes.

"Jess, someone's taking my truck now. The cops won't get here in time."

He snaked his free hand around her slender waist and kissed her on the forehead. "Don't look so worried. It's probably just kids. One look at this…" he raised the sword, his bicep bulging from all the curls he did "… and they'll run like hell." Or so he hoped.

A tear trickled down her cheek. He delicately brushed it away with his thumb, then kissed her again. Finally, he pulled away and stormed down the stairs taking two at a time. The twenty-eight-inch steel blade glinted in the darkness.

He shot across the oak-floored hallway and grabbed the brass front door handle.

At the top of the stairs, Jessica was now just a dark figure looming out of the gloom, her long white Knicks T-shirt like a shroud.

She whispered, "Please, David." Her voice broke as she fought to control her fear. "It's not worth it."

Stabbing his sword at the closed bedroom door to her left, he said in a hushed voice, "Lock yourself in with the kids. And call 911 again."

Jessica cupped her hands to her face and stood shaking. She was understandably terrified. And this in her own home. Her own goddamn home. No asshole was going to get away with doing that to her.

He stabbed at the room, once more. "Go, Jessica. Now."

Looking at him, she shuffled backward toward the bedroom door.

He forced a smile. "Everything's gonna be just fine. Promise."

Drawing a huge, shaky breath, he looked down at his sword. The blade glistened in the moonlight filtering through the opaque glass in the front door. A baseball bat? A baseball bat was for pussies. He hadn't gone into debt up to his balls for some lowlife scum to wreck their last chance at happiness. If someone was screwing with his new truck, he'd slice them in two.

He glanced back one last time at Jessica as she peeked through the half-closed door of the kids' bedroom.

David turned and ripped open the front door. He stormed out into the night.

A garage stood at the end of their shadow-strewn driveway. An open garage. A garage that he'd earlier double-checked he'd locked to protect his new truck after he'd reversed it in.

The faltering moonlight unveiled a shadow at the steering wheel.

David raised his sword. Pointed it at the shadow. Shouted. "Get the fuck out of my truck, or I'll slice your fucking legs off!"

The figure did not leave the vehicle.

David marched toward his truck. He slashed his sword through the air, its blade gleaming with deadly sharpness in the moonlight. Hell, had this guy picked the wrong truck and the wrong man to screw with. "Out of the fucking truck, asshole!"

Footsteps scraped on the concrete drive behind him.

He spun around. Sword raised. But something heavy smacked into the side of his head.

David crashed into the cold, rock-hard ground like a sack of amputated body parts.

He gasped for breath.

On his back, he reached up. For what, he didn't know.

His thoughts spinning, he blinked to try to bring the world back into focus.

Groggily, he pushed himself over onto his stomach. Muscles shaking with the effort, he heaved up onto his hands and knees.

He swayed as he felt his head. Strangely, there was no pain. But the world was sluggish and blurred, sounds and images melting into an indecipherable mass of noise and colors.

He shook his head to try to clear it so that he could think, so he could figure out what had happened and what to do about it. And that's when the pain started – a pounding like someone was caving in his skull with a baseball bat.

Grimacing, he turned his head to one side as if he could escape the hammering by moving away from it.

A roaring engine cracked the still night.

He raised his heavy, heavy head. Swung it to his left.

Headlights blasted into his face. Then, they reared straight at him.

Closer...

Closer...

Mustering the last of his strength, he scrambled to dodge out of the way.

But the metal beast clipped him. Like a rampaging bull, it spun him and slammed him against the house wall.

David crumpled to the ground.

Face down on the cold concrete, blood oozing from his mouth, he saw red lights cut through the darkness. Brake lights.

Squealing tires clawed at the ground and then raced back toward him.

What… What were they doing?

No… No, they couldn't be…

He wanted to push up. But couldn't. He wanted to roll out of the way. But couldn't. He wanted to live. But…

His truck careened straight at him.

No.

Nooo.

NOOO!

Chapter 02

Lying on room 1422's tan couch, an 'L' shaped beast that would consume half her living room, Tess Williams heard voices in the hotel corridor outside. Boisterous male voices.

Wearing nitrile gloves to complement her naughty nurse costume, she pulled her flimsy outfit higher so her red panties were on view. On many an occasion, guys had told her she had great legs. With the amount of exercise she did, they'd better be damn great. But no amount of training ever did anything about her bony knees. Hell, she hated her knees.

She pushed her boobs up to ensure her cleavage was as full as possible through the gaping white cotton uniform and then spread the hair of her long blond wig over them.

Her boobs? Men liked them too. But men were easily satisfied. Given the choice, she'd go up a bra cup to a C.

But then was any woman ever happy with her boobs?

None that she'd ever known.

That said, she'd never slept with a guy who didn't want an extra inch or two on his dick.

Why was no one ever happy with what they had? Why did they always want more?

The door opened. As did her thighs – whoever entered would get a nice clear shot of her red satin gusset. If that didn't bring on an instant hard-on, this guy was a eunuch.

Half in the room, his bald head facing into the corridor still, the man waved. "Pass my appreciation to Big Frank, guys. Good of him to set me up like this. Tell him I'm looking forward to catching up tomorrow."

He shut the door and turned.

Froze. Mouth agape.

He stared at her. "Whoa."

Tess smiled. "Big Frank says 'Hi'."

Eyes wide, the man all but drooled saliva onto his pot belly, a belly so big she'd curse if he waddled onto a bus and the only spare seat was beside her.

With a press of the remote control, the light from the gold-colored chandelier dimmed. Tess tossed the remote aside and beckoned him with a single finger curl. She'd slept with a lot of men. A lot of men. But this guy was special. The pleasure this lard-ass was going to give her, she'd remember him till the day she died.

Baldy stumbled toward her, kicking off his shoes and ripping off his jacket. He tossed his wristwatch, what looked like a Rolex, onto the onyx table. "Big Frank said I'd get what I deserved for keeping my mouth shut, but you...?" He crashed down beside her on the couch and pawed her left breast like an apprentice baker kneading his first lump of dough.

She tossed her hair back. "You think this is good, wait till you see what I've got for you in the bedroom."

Baldy smiled. "You've got something special planned?"

"Baby, you'll forget every birthday you've ever had." She cupped his crotch. There was a bulge, but nothing any woman would ever rush to tell her girlfriends about.

She said, "So, how long is it since this bad boy had himself some hot snatch?"

"Three years, ten months, twenty-eight days."

"Hell, I'm surprised you haven't burst already."

"Honey, after four years of a cellmate with a face like a gorilla and the breath to match, I'm so hard a truckload of horse tranquilizers wouldn't stop me fucking you till Tuesday."

"Then what are we waiting for?" She led him by the hand to the bedroom.

Once there, she smiled at him. "I hear you like it interesting. Can I interest you in any of my charms?" She whipped a silk cover off a gold chest at the foot of the super king-size bed.

Baldy gasped at a collection of objects which could be used for twisted sex, among them a blindfold; a ball-gag; handcuffs with various lengths of chain; a leather strap for sharpening cutthroat razors; a scalpel; a hunting knife; a switchblade; a black strap-on dildo; a whip.

Baldy moaned as he ran a hand along the full length of the ten-inch strap-on dildo, then trailed it over the knives. "Oh, yeah."

Tess ripped open her uniform. She gently drew his hand away from the table as she leaned up to kiss him. "I want you to use me like you used those other women."

"Like I used them?"

"Uh-huh." She unfastened the clasp on the front of her red satin bra.

He pulled back slightly and nodded to the table. "And I can use anything?"

"Go for it, baby."

"Even the knives?"

"For what Big Frank's paying me, even the knives. But only three cuts, baby. And not the face. Okay?"

A grin spread across his face as if the master of ceremonies had just called out his name at an awards dinner for Sex God of the Year.

Tess said, "They say you banged some of those women so hard, afterward they were only good for ten-buck hooks in Chinatown."

Squeezing her breasts, he said, "You better believe it, you dirty little whore." He squashed them together, making her cleavage as deep as possible. He licked along it.

Why did men squash breasts like that? She groaned as if it was pleasurable. It was as if they thought boobs were made out of Silly Putty and if they pressed hard enough they could make one big one. Did guys really think women liked it?

"Tell me," she said. "Tell me how you used them. Make me wet."

"Oh, hell, I like you." He squeezed her left nipple between his thumb and forefinger. Squeezed hard as if testing if it were ripe.

She bit her lip to stop from crying out.

He rolled her nipple around. "There was one girl, maybe fourteen – Romanian, Bulgarian, some crap like that – a tiny little thing. Man, was she tight. What every guy dreams of. I fucked her so hard the doc had to put in fifteen sutures."

His fingers slid over the three-inch scar on her left side where she'd been slashed with a kitchen knife on the recent Leo McMannus job. Her body was a tool she needed to complete her work. A tool she needed to keep in prime condition. A tool prone to damage. While blade work made Baldy hard, it was a turn off for most guys, so like she had with all her other scars, she'd have to get that latest imperfection fixed.

Baldy kissed her left breast. He ran his tongue from one nipple to the other. Admiring her boobs, he said, "So, not your first time playing games, huh?"

He was looking at the three faded round scars on the underside of her left breast, scars about the size of the end of a cigarette.

She smiled. "A memento from a past life."

That she wouldn't be getting fixed. That reminded her of why she had to do what she did. Why she could never stop. Because if she did, there'd be no one else to care, no one else to see justice done.

He slathered his tongue around her right nipple again.

Tess moaned. "Oh, baby, I want you now."

207

He stared at her breasts. "Man, I'm going to do you so hard you won't walk for a month."

He pushed her down on the bed. Then went to the table.

"I'm wet for you, baby. Don't leave me too long."

Studying the table of toys, he said, "Oh, don't worry your pretty little head. Daddy's gonna give it to you long and hard."

He picked up the hunting knife. Turned it. Watched it glisten. Smiled.

He stood over her, eyes wide, breath fast.

"Come on, baby. Do it." She licked her lips.

His gaze roamed her body, then, predictably, fell back onto her breasts. He leaned down, knife raised. As the tip drew closer and closer to her flesh, he smiled wider and wider. "Yeah, I'm gonna make you squeal all kinds of ways, whore."

His eyes widened with glee as he pulled the knife back for the first cut.

***

"Great story with an excellent plot and lots of action."
5 STARS – P. Flanders

"Great action, fight scenes, and story line."
5 STARS – Elizabeth Robb

"This series just keeps getting better with each book."
5 STARS – Mary Grady

Continue the adventure now with this link:
http://stevenleebooks.com/jpwb

Free Library of Books

Thank you for reading *Angel of Darkness*. To show my appreciation of my readers, I wrote a second series of books exclusively for you – each *Angel of Darkness* book has its own *Black File*, so there's a free library for you to collect and enjoy (books you cannot get anywhere else).

Start Your FREE Library with *Black File 02*.
http://stevenleebooks.com/fn8p

This also entitles you to get my VIP readers newsletter every month, with some combination of:

- news about my books
- special deals/freebies from me or my writer friends
- opportunities to help choose book titles and covers
- anecdotes about the writing life, or just life itself
- behind-the-scenes peeks at what's in the works.

Angel of Darkness Series

Book 01 – Kill Switch

This Amazon #1 Best Seller explodes with pulse-pounding action and heart-stopping thrills, as Tess Williams rampages across Eastern Europe in pursuit of a gang of sadistic kidnappers.

Book 02 – Angel of Darkness

Set in Manhattan, Tess hunts a merciless killer on a mission from God in a story bursting with high-octane action and nail-biting suspense.

Book 03 – Blood Justice

Blood Justice erupts with the intrigue, betrayal and red-hot action surrounding a senseless murder. Thrust into the deadly world of crime lords and guns-for-hire, only Tess can unveil the killer in this gripping action-fest.

Book 04 – Midnight Burn

An unstoppable killing-machine, Tess demands justice for crimes, whatever the cost. But even 'unstoppable' machines have weaknesses. Discover Tess's as she hunts a young woman's fiendish killer.

Book 05 – Mourning Scars

Crammed with edge-of-your-seat action, suspense, and vengeance, this adventure slams Tess into the heart of a gang shooting and reveals the nightmare that drove her to become a justice-hungry killer.

Book 06 – Predator Mine

Bursting with nerve-shredding intrigue, this page-turner plunges Tess into the darkest of crimes. And dark crimes deserve dark justice. Discover just how dark a hero can be when Tess hunts a child killer.

Book 07 – Nightmare's Rage

If someone killed somebody you loved, how far would you go to get justice? How dark would be too dark? How violent too violent? Vengeance-driven Tess is about to find out in an electrifying action extravaganza.

Book 08 – Shanghai Fury

Tess Williams is a killer. Cold. Brutal. Unstoppable. In a white-knuckle tale of murder, mayhem, and betrayal, discover how her story begins, how an innocent victim becomes a merciless killing-machine.

Book 09 – Black Dawn

Everything ends. Including a life of pain, hardship, and violence. Tess has sacrificed endlessly to protect the innocent by hunting those that prey upon them. Now, it's time to build a new life for herself. But a news report changes everything.

Book 10 – Die Forever

A brutal gang is terrorizing NYC. Tess's hunt takes her to one of the deadliest places on the planet, for one of her deadliest battles. How will she get out alive?

About Steve N. Lee

Steve lives in Yorkshire, in the north of England, with his partner Ania and two cats who adopted them.

Picture rugged, untamed moorland with Cathy running into Heathcliff's arms – that's Yorkshire! Well, without the running. (Picture jet-black bundles of fur – that's their cats.)

He's studied a number of martial arts, is a certified SCUBA diver, and speaks 10 languages enough to get by. And he loves bacon sandwiches smothered in brown sauce.

Use the link below to learn more – some of it true, some of it almost true, and some of it, well, who really knows? Why not decide for yourself?

http://stevenleebooks.com/a5w5